Books by Jay Erickson

## The Blood Wizard Chronicles-

*Pariah*
*Recrean*

## The Wayfarer Prince Saga-

*Stormwind*
*Dark Consort*
*Pononga*
*Hollow Omen* (coming soon!)

## Other Works-

*Barrow of Lies*
*The Wild Tide* (co-authored with J.P. Strohm)

Books by **J.P.** Strohm

**Mark of the Raven Series-**

*Broken Order*
*Veil of Resolve* (coming soon!)

**Other Works-**

*The Wild Tide* (co-authored with Jay Erickson)

# PRAISE FOR

## *Mark of the Raven- Broken Order*

"In his solo debut, J.P. Strohm introduces us to the force of nature that is Raven. He captures the essence of a grim world in the wake of warfare, as well as the courage of those willing risk it all to do what is right. A gritty read for those who like traces of realism as well as humanity in their fantasy."

-Jay Erickson, author of *The Blood Wizard Chronicles*

"A gripping journey through the eyes of an elite warrior – the mysterious Exactors and their history continues to evolve, and keeps readers on the edge of their seats. Strohm takes Erickson's world into new horizons as he returns to the setting of a much-loved Erickson story in Stormwind. However, this is not just a tribute, but a new entry into Exactor lore, and a satisfying one at that."

-Anastasia M. Trekles, author of *The Chronicles of M'gistryn*

J.P. Strohm's *Broken Order* is fantasy action-adventure mystery, that follows a young woman named Raven, an exactor from the Jasian Enclave. As a member of the famed 105th Northern Contingent, Raven and her team hunt down magical threats that they've combated for nearly a decade. J.P. Strohm tells the tale from another angle for the fans of the *Wayfarer Prince Saga* – introducing even more layers into an ever growing complex realm. This is a well-done addition to the world of Kuldarr.

-Jason Bigart, award-winning director for *Dark Trepidation*

# The Wayfarer Prince Saga-Pononga

"Jay Erickson's writing is extraordinarily lucid and vivid. He entwines the story-line and the characters with uncanny detail and pragmatism, it makes you think you're truly watching Stormwind and his exploits! I found myself pondering what would happen next, and couldn't wait to get home from work to continue reading it! I highly recommend it!"
-George Kramer, author of the *Arcadis Fantasy Series*

# The Wayfarer Prince Saga-Dark Consort

"The character of Stormwind is aptly named, as he floats in to people's lives and shakes them up in more ways than one! The author weaves a complex tale marrying classic heroism and mystery elements with modern ideas in a complex fantasy world. Stormwind's character acts as a catalyst, moving the action and keeping the reader guessing as to what might come next. Follow Stormwind's path and get a deep and exciting look into the culture, intrigue, and emotions of a unique race of Elves through this new novella from Jay Erickson."
-Anastasia Trekles, author of *Core*

# The Wayfarer Prince Saga-Stormwind

"*Stormwind* is an intense, character-driven melodrama that never ceases to be entertaining. It's heroes are immediately likeable and the action is vivid, but it has just enough substance to make the reader think. Plus, it has so many plot twists both M. Night Shyamalan and Christopher Nolan are jealous!"
-Nathan Marchand, author of *Pandora's Box* and co-creator of *Children of the Wells*

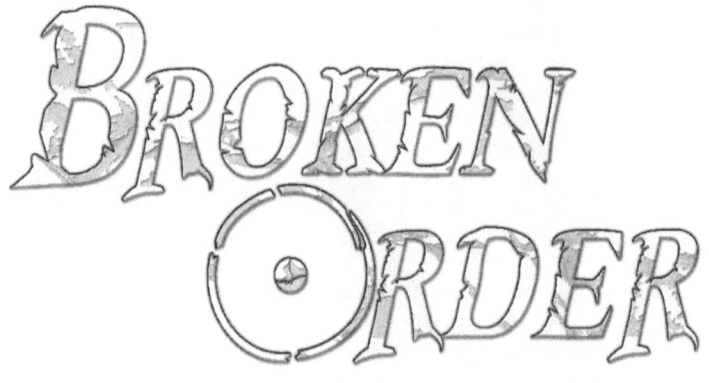

# Broken Order

A MARK OF THE RAVEN NOVEL

BY:

# J. P. STROHM

HALSBREN
PUBLISHING, LLC

THE EXACTORS: TALES FROM THE CITADEL
MARK OF THE RAVEN BOOK ONE:
BROKEN ORDER

Copy Editor Kathleen LaSelle
Content Editor Jay Erickson
Cover design by Jay Erickson
Art by Stefan Keller
Raven by Deborah Koenig
Cover Photography by Marcus J. Ranum
Cover Model Amber Gangi
Additional art royalty free by FreeVector.Com, and Pixabay.Com
Published By: Halsbren Publishing LLC. *La Porte, IN. 46350*
ISBN **978-1-942958-15-4**
Made in the United States of America.

# DEDICATION

To my daughter, Crystal, who took a pregenerated character with a repeating crossbow, and infused it into a woman of pure attitude. I hope that I can show you one hell of a strong female character as an example to never give up.

-J.P. Strohm
Author

# TABLE OF CONTENTS

# INTRODUCTION

**EXACTORS** – they come from all walks of life. From vagrants to war heroes, from priests to sorcerers, from criminals to law enforcers, they come from everywhere seeking a chance at a better life. Even those from the noblest of houses sometimes look to establish their own legacy.

Exactors are the Jasian Enclave's dirty little secret, contractors whose duty it is to complete the missions that the Church cannot openly admit to doing, or if they need an expendable asset. The range of such missions varies widely, as does the unique skills of the Exactors.

Within these pages, is one of the rare chronicled exploits of an Exactor. It has been pieced together by recently found documents, billing statements, shipping manifests, trusted sources, and even hearsay. This event which is code named **Broken Order**; for your better understanding, is loosely tied to the widely known historical event, **Stormwind**.

For the sake of clarity, it will be labeled with a generalized date when it is believed to have taken place, and a rough estimate of how about how close in proximity it was to the event, **Stormwind**.

It is important to know that not all actions performed by the Exactors are nefarious, nor are they benevolent, but within these pages is a mixture of both. It shows the flexibility of the Exactor, and why the Jasian Enclave needs them so...

-Aria Càidh
Chronicler of Jasian History

**4855 E.o.E**

---

**AGOT**

# PRELUDE
*By: Jay Erickson*

# 1

It was a late night – of that he was certain – though the very sky was scorched hot with auburn light, like the world was cast in the burnished hues of a setting sun. This was no sunset that lit the night sky, however. It was fire.

The boomtown known as Agot burned.

Purist Commander Aodhfin Bray rode with purpose; behind him, like a roll of thunder on the horizon, the 105th Northern Territories Contingent surged across the farmlands like a wild tide. Steelclad hooves hammered hardened clay, sending fragments and dust in great plumes into the amber seared night.

Screams and the clash of iron echoed across the highlands over the roar of fire. Above all the din of chaos, Aodhfin Bray heard the hollow reverberations of a gong. This was no burning granary – this was a raid.

Aodhfin Bray leapt his steed over a small wooden fence of someone's farmland. He slid through aureate wheat fields, cutting a massive swath in Agot's source of food. That mattered little at the moment, for the lives within Agot itself were all that mattered to him.

They entered the edge of the trade town, where the streets were cluttered with the dead and wounded. Blood tattooed the building's walls like perverse graffiti. Women clutched their babes and ran screaming out of the streets like crazed livestock. They all streamed west, up to a long flat structure high on the horizon line – the home of the Order of the Sacred Fist.

"By the Maker," his second-in-command bellowed as he recoiled at the sight of so much carnage.

"Hold the line together, Amháin," Bray commanded. He then felt his second wheel about, shouting orders to his closing contingent.

Bray's eyes danced across the branded landscape searching for survivors they could aid, but even more so, he was searching for the raiders. So much desolation wracked this town in so short a time that it must be an organized force that attacked. It had to be the work of Ambrosia. But who could she have recruited that would be capable of such butchery? Malten? Surely the nation of desert mages wouldn't stoop to slaughtering innocent traders and farmers. They were much too proud for that. So, who?

Bray watched shadows shift in the blistering glow of the burning buildings. What he saw made his blood go cold, even amongst the torrential heat that assailed him. "It cannot be," he muttered aloud.

Five men were engaged in a fight for their lives. Four against one, two of them were Agot guard, one clearly a civilian, and another had to be one of the monks from the nearby monastery.

Their opponent, though, was nothing short of a Wilder.

The Wilder towered over the others, casting even the tallest of them in his eclipse. He was at least seven feet tall and almost three feet wide at the shoulders. He wore no armor, nor clothing, instead wearing only the skins and furs of the monsters of the Wilds on his body. Bray could make out what looked like sabertooth tiger skulls on the massive man's hands, and the skin of a reptile running over the barbarian's knees and feet. His thighs, chest, and arms were bare, showing thick, hardened muscles and a myriad of scars bred from countless struggles. His face was hidden behind the visage of a basilisk's skull, a terrible lizard that dwelt within the Wild lands. It was said that the beast could kill by its very breath, or even with a look, and this man was wearing its skull as a trophy... surely a testament to his skill in combat.

"She's turned the Wilders..." Even as he said the words to himself, he could hardly believe it. This wasn't going to be a raid for wealth, or crops, or even slaves. This was going to be a slaughter.

Before thinking to issue orders to his men, he pushed the horse into the throng of escapees, intent on trying to aid the battlers locked in mortal combat with the beast of the Wilds. Behind him, he could hear Amháin calling out to him for instruction, but still Bray rode. He needed to help them – the last time he encountered Wilders, people he'd loved died.

However, he could not gallop directly for them, for risk of trampling innocent women and children beneath his horse's weight. He could only watch, and pray to the Maker as he closed the gap that he would be able to help in time. Ahead, the Wild Man handled the four men with the ease of a veteran. He swung his cumbersome battleaxe with ruthless efficiency. The Wilder overmatched the two guards before they even truly engaged him. Within seconds the two were cut down, their life's blood cooking on the walls of the nearby burning structures. The Wilder fought against the blistering crimson incalescence, his own battle fervor blazing as hot as the charring buildings around him. There was no regard for having taken the men's lives.

Still, the monk and the civilian fought on, and Bray leapt off his horse, drawing his warhammer in practiced motion. He glanced down to make certain the buckles of his round shield were fastened tight against his forearm. They were. He ran forward intent on saving at least those two men.

The monk was truly talented, and Bray admired the mettle of the man for not losing his courage in the face of such insurmountable odds. The monk dodged the axe blows easily, maneuvering quickly between the openings the Wilder created, to strike him in a flurry of ruthless blows. Welts formed across the giant's body where the monk's fists and feet fell like mace collisions. Still the monk's crushing impact did not seem to faze the Wilder in the slightest; if anything, it emboldened the savage to fight even harder.

Bray managed to reach the civilian's side just as the giant axe whistled through the air for his head. The battle-hardened Purist slid his shield up between the Wilder and the civilian fighting with a sickle and the crack of the powerful axe against his shield arm sent him straight into the wall. The air exploded from his lungs in a great gust and embers flickered before him, threatening to steal his consciousness.

"Maker," he gasped, then his gaze fell quickly to the man he saved. His face, as white as linen, showed realization that he was only a hair's breadth from near decapitation. Instead of dropping his farmer's tool and fleeing, the civilian screamed in rage and swung recklessly at the Wilder. *What a cornered man will do to protect his home*, Bray thought. He hooked the crescent weapon over the beast's wrist, drawing a line across an exposed forearm. Like the blossoming of a new rose, the flesh parted and a bloom of red-hot blood surged from rent muscle.

Bray recovered, moving forward, the scent of his charred tabard from leaning against the burning building pierced his nostrils. He hefted his hammer and engaged the threat.

Combat is a measure of patience, an eye for detail, trust in your training, and a bucketload of pure luck. Everyone had a coin for what would be their one trip to the end of days, but it was only a matter of when it was collected. Some merely paid the toll quicker than others.

Bray slammed the flat of his warhammer into his steel shield. The clamor reverberated down his already numb arm, but gave him a measure of personal fortitude for what was to come. Sweat slickened his gambeson inside his platemail armor from the intense heat, and he felt the moisture bead and pool on his brow.

"We take him, together, as one," he commanded the monk and civilian.

"Yes," the monk answered calmly. An equal, but not as strong reply came from the man with the sickle.

Bray stared hard into the gruesome mask of the Wilder. Hazel eyes glared back... but they were perplexed. The Wilders had clearly not anticipated seeing Purists here. They were the only thing that might save this town tonight.

"For the Maker!" Bray bellowed, and he charged.

The monk was beside him in an instant, with the farmer only a second behind. The Wilder, slick with sweat, uttered a beastly roar and swung his axe masterfully, but Bray intercepted the axe head with his shield. The blow thundered through him, rattling his teeth, and driving him to a knee. That was okay though, for Bray long ago realized that battle wasn't a single man's engagement, but a team's – something the lone barbarian would quickly learn in the end.

By letting the Wilder fully follow through with the attack, it slowed him by a heartbeat to react to the other threats, like the monk. Fluid, like moving water, the monk swept up and over the Wilder's reach, toward his head, driving the tips of his fingers up under the bone helm and into the soft throat of the monster. Bray heard the crackle of cartilage as the monk's fingers pushed through.

Bray stared into the mask once more, deep into the Wilder's soul. He understood that the barbarian knew something was wrong, but was confused. Likely it was only a pinch, but now he couldn't breathe. A gasp escaped the ossein visor, and the Wilder dropped down to his knee, clutching at his throat. Bray wasted no time, nor permitted the beast to suffer, no matter how monstrous it might have been. He stood swiftly and with all his might he brought his hammer down on the basilisk's skull helm. Bone fragmented as the hammer passed through, finding the skull of the giant beneath. A second layer of bone turned into debris as the Wilder's skull caved in.

He withdrew his hammer, and the massive man collapsed before them, twitching the last vestiges of his life out onto the smoldering earth.

Bray turned to the monk and civilian. "Quickly, where is everyone rallying? Can you tell me?"

"The... the Drunken Priest," the civilian muttered. "It's where most of the townsolk were told to flee to if they couldn't escape to the monastery."

"Where is it?"

The monk pointed to the northwest. "Center of town." There was a look of urgency in his eyes, though.

"What is it?"

The monk pointed east, "I saw my Master of the Order of the Sacred Fist heading east with an elf, looking for her missing son. Last I saw they were fighting a woman that was wielding magic. I came to find help. I cannot do battle with a Creationist; I am no master."

"Ambrosia…" Bray growled. For seven winters now, he'd hunted that sorceress. She'd been his sole purpose in all that time, but she was always one step ahead of him. Perhaps his luck had finally turned.

The 105th Contingent caught up and began to surround the trio. "Orders, ser?" Amháin asked.

Aodhfin Bray wasted no time. "Divide into three groups. I want Purist Ceartas to lead the majority of the contingent through the heart of the town, to a tavern called the Drunken Priest. They will be our vanguard, striking at the heart of the Wilders and rendering aid when and where they can." He directed Amháin's attention to the civilian with the sickle. "This man will be Ceartas' guide. Amháin, you build a perimeter force, as fast a group as you can manage, and help keep safe passage open for the civilians making their way to the monastery. Engage any Wilders trying to hunt them down."

"Very good, ser," Amháin told the Purist Commander. "I assume you are leading the third group?"

"Yes," Bray all but snarled, "give me Raven, Varthstone, Rhall, and Dwyn, all on horses." Bray looked to the monk, who nodded at him. With righteous fervor he added, "We're hunting ourselves a sorceress tonight."

**2**

Amháin stared at the wreckage of smoldering shops and homes all around him. Hours passed since their arrival, and they did all they could to repel this… attack, if it could be called such. It was more like a massacre. What was the point?

As far as Amháin could learn, the Wilders came only to kill. In fact, his memory was permanently stained this night from the extermination squads he and his group eliminated, many shortly after they butchered children. Children! And for what? What?!

His tired eyes fell to the last bastion of Agot, this Drunken Priest tavern. Shrouded bodies lined the streets – covered from head to toe in the linens taken from the tavern, many already beginning to stain pink. Too many of those still mounds were tiny – too tiny. Amháin felt his eyes watering at the indignation of it all. He spit on the ground in disgust and wiped at his face, lest the men see his tears.

A clamor of voices calling out for their Purist Commander brought Amháin around. He could see Bray now, his blue tabard sodden with blood. Over his shoulders was a high elf, and following at his side was a remarkably beautiful young woman with wild black tresses and smoldering brown eyes. Those eyes were worn and despondent. It was clear she, too, had recently been crying. This stranger with Bray wore the gi of a monk, clothing with which he was now all too familiar with.

Amháin saluted his commander, and wearily, Bray bobbed his head in acknowledgement.

Bray's voice was as tired as the rest of him. "Give me an estimate on casualties, Amháin."

"For us," Amháin said, "two."

Bray nodded in resignation. "And the town?"

"First estimates are putting it around thirty…" Amháin stalled. He felt Bray's piercing blue eyes on him, so he continued. "Most are children, commander."

Bray cursed audibly.

Amháin almost hesitated in the asking. "Ambrosia?"

Bray shook his head no. "There was a sorceress, that's for certain. She's in the wind now."

Amháin spit again, this time not to cover his tears, but in loathing. For almost a decade, this wretch had avoided their judgement. He stifled his anger, had to believe that the Maker had a purpose for this – even for Ambrosia. Amháin took note of the elf Bray was holding then. "Is that a prisoner?"

"Person of interest," the Purist Commander countered. "He stood up to the Wilder leader and the sorceress with this monk."

"Was the sorceress Ambrosia?"

Bray bit his lip, mulling it over. "I don't know, maybe."

"And that elf will have answers?"

Bray shrugged, which proved difficult with the weight of the unconscious elf hanging on him. "He's the best lead we've got at the moment. Apparently, they were here for her kid."

Amháin reevaluated the woman, who seemed awfully young to have a child. He pursed his lips. "The elf the husband?"

"Didn't ask yet," Bray answered. "I intend to get down to the bottom of this – namely, why Ambrosia wanted her son."

Amháin nodded, his gaze once again falling to the tiny canvas wrapped bodies in rows in the street. "Yes, do find out why, ser."

"I will." Bray looked to the horizon where the monastery could just be seen through the thick haze of black smoke saturating the town as people put out the fires. "Amháin, you're in charge until I return. Provide aid to these people, set up patrols to search for any pockets of Wilder skirmishers that might be hiding, and look for survivors. If you can spare the manpower, perhaps help put out all these damned fires."

Amháin saluted. "As you will, ser."

With a free hand, Bray saluted back. "We're close this time, Amháin, I can feel it in my bones. As soon as I learn anything, I'll be in touch."

"Yes, ser."

Bray turned to leave, and it was clear he had one more thing on his mind. He looked back to Amháin. "Purist?"

"Ser?"

"Try not to be too hard on Raven."

Amháin's lip curled in revulsion.

"Yeah," Bray answered, "that's what I figured."

4855 E.o.E

ONE WEEK LATER...

# CHAPTER I

# 1

The sky around the Agontill Highland hillsides was still filled with the wisps of grey smoke. It was an ever-present reminder of the burning of Agot, and the horror of the attack from the 'Wilds'.

A walled structure stood firmly off in the distance, about a mile away. It was a monastery just to the northwest, and it seemed to be the only building to escape the assault on the town.

To her east, about one hundred yards away, there was a small outcropping of makeshift fencing. Made of wood and stone it stood away from the town. Processions of people were making their way into it carrying a small pine box, with mourners following behind. The box was so tiny that the occupant could be none other than a young child. Another innocent caught in the slaughter of the attack.

The mourners, dressed in black, with the women covering their faces in veils, were hunched over from the enormity of the loss. Some of the men were at the women's sides to hold them and steady their walk. Even then, she saw one stumble, and try to back up away from the cemetery overwhelmed by grief.

A young man attending her stopped with the woman, whispered gently, and helped her press forward stoically with the others. Her cries resonated on the wind like a melancholy lullaby. A bard's tale of an adventure that did not have a happy ending.

She stood there for a moment, at her sentry post, watching in silence before eventually turning her gaze back to the southeast toward the Trade Road. This main artery led to Ethens and the Lugos Mountains. Moreover it led away from all of this pain.

She adjusted her platemail helmet. While it obscured her features and covered most of her shoulder length brownish-red hair, her green gaze was not obstructed by the overcast shadow of the head covering. Just inside that protective shell she could feel her petite nose just barely grazing the nose guard. They had sized it perfectly for her, of course. Her thin lips and narrow jaw line were the only things exposed through the opening, and that was the most anyone saw of her face.

The rest of her armor was as fitted as her helmet. It hugged her five-foot-eight-inch frame, but not so tightly that it limited her agility in combat. It was still dusty and dented with scuffs, all visible signs of battle.

Overlaid upon the armor was a light blue tabard with a circumpunct symbol. The emblem was meant for one under the service of the Jasian Enclave.

In armaments she wore her personal throwing axe on her right hip and countered the weight with a longsword on her left. These crude implements were not her preferred choice of weapon however. She felt her favored possession's weight resting against the center of her back. The sight of it often gave the uninitiated pause. For what they saw was the wooden figure of a contorted face with black eyes and white, sharp teeth. Various tribal etchings trailed down the weapon's stock. It looked like a monster, but what it really was was a crossbow facing downward. It was ornately decorated and unique to her alone. A one of a kind gift she received a long time ago. For this special crossbow held a chamber off to its left side, set at a forty-five degree angle. This beast of a weapon held five chambers of quarrels ready to dole out death. The thought of its use, only recently, brought the touch of a smile to her face. It was a stark thing in comparison with the macabe scene around her.

The crunch of feet on gravel alerted her to someone approaching from behind. The woman turned around just as the man called out, "Raven, a word please."

The sentry named Raven sighed and slowly approached the younger man of his late twenties. He was well built, and tall for his nationality. He, like she, was a warrior who was clad in similar platemail armor. Unlike her however, he favored a large battle mace and a kite shield, all adorned in the classic Jaslan Enclave symbology; a circle within a circle – the circumpunct.

When she was about ten feet from him she stopped and placed her right arm across her chest. Raven bowed slightly from the shoulders and lowered her head and eyes to the ground, "Purist Amháin, how can I serve the Maker and the Enclave?"

He returned the greeting, and announced, "The Maker requires your particular skills that will allow you entrance into his presence and redemption of your transgressions… again."

"To which of these skills do you refer, Purist Amháin? Is it my arms or at range?" she asked as she stood up straighter.

"Maybe both, but first you must find what it is the Maker and the Enclave wishes you to locate."

"Tracking then."

Amháin turned back towards Agot, "Walk with me, Exactor." His words sounded like a request, yet Raven knew it was otherwise.

She nodded and began her walk next to the purist. She stayed to his right, only half a step behind. They began the trek down the small hill. Shortly after, another armor-clad purist ran past them up the slope to take her place as sentinel to the town and the Trade Road.

Raven walked quietly next to the large man, waiting for him to speak. She was an exactor, and generally she wasn't allowed to to speak to a purist unless first spoken to.

She knew her role well. Exactors were specialists contracted by the Enclave to do their dirty work. This gave the church plausible deniability in case an exactor committed an atrocity that didn't exactly follow in line with the religious nation's way of thinking. Raven's contractual obligation was like many exactors with criminal backgrounds - indentured servitude or death.

Before assuming the role of exactor, Raven was part of a group that stole something that was claimed 'could not be stolen while within the monolithic walls of the Citadel'. It resided within the very seat of the Gurgen Kingdom. The Supreme Pontiff's – Rod of the Maker. A legendary symbol of the Jasian Enclave, and only touched by the men of the god himself.

They had it for exactly three minutes.

Arrest, battery, and subsequent trial followed. During the trial, when asked why Raven did it she replied sarcastically, "I just wanted to be the only woman in the realm that could say I held the Maker's rod." She tadded a gesture of sucking on it, to add insult to injury.

The uproar that followed amongst the judiciary alone was almost worth her execution. Never, to Raven's knowledge, had such holy men used more colorful language. Her defense council pleaded to have her spared due to her unique skill set. She would serve the Maker and it was, after all, the duty of all purists to convert the unconvertible. So the choice was given to her and the group involved. – all chose service.

That was the last Raven ever saw of them. The group were all divided to separate purists units shortly afterwards. That was seven winters ago.

Seven long winters, in Purist Aodhfin Bray's 105th Northen contingent, hunting a sorceress named Ambrosia. A hunt that led her to this moment, and this town – Agot. A town that, when they arrived, they found in shambles from an attack by the Wildmen from the south.

Strangely, soon after their arrival, Purist Commander Aodhfin Bray left Amháin in charge of the contingent and set out with a monk from the Order of the Sacred Fist and a High Elf guide into the very depths of the Wilds. It was more than a little peculiar.

Amháin did not disclose the nature of Bray's mission, but informed all that they needed to continue to search Agot for the sorceress, or any evidence thereof.

That was a week ago.

Raven's thoughts were interrupted by Amháin. "It seems that another Master of the Order of the Sacred Fist is missing. There is some discord amongst the order. We believe that the master was assisting in the defense of the town and may not be accounted for yet."

"How is that?" she asked as she looked toward the town and the monastery off in the distance. She glanced back to the purist. Raven never lost step with him. "How can they not notice him gone for this long?"

"According to eye witnesses, Master Ferric was last seen on the west side of town taking on four Wildmen. When the enemy withdrew it was assumed he was still there attending to the injured. The monks said he was well known in that section and had acquaintances there. He may have stayed to make sure they were in satisfactory condition," Amháin answered. "The order can function with two masters no problem. Now there is but one…"

Raven noticed as they approached the town's main entry road two other exactors and another purist were there. They seemed to be waiting for them.

She recognized the other purist immediately. It was Ceartas, Amháin's temporary second-in-command. He was a battle-tested warrior and skilled healer with Creative magic – which was rare for the men of the Enclave to be Curates. He, like many Purists, preferred blunt weaponry. His was a large silver mace complimented with a small round shield. His armor glinted in the sunlight. Ceartas was well known for keeping his gear clean at all times. He once claimed, "The Maker allows me to blind his enemies with 'His' brilliance to serve righteous justice to those who are not of the Maker's will, or in repentance of their sins."

It was no secret that he would spend hours cleaning and polishing the gear after every battle, only taking a break for sustenance or sleep. Some even said that when healed by him on the frontlines, "It was like the Maker himself was in attendance within the glow of light around him." Many found the experience so uplifting that right after the healing they would jump back into the fray of battle to prove themselves to the Maker and 'His' will.

Raven could understand just by looking at the charismatic tall man. Most people from Gurgen had dark hair and swarthy skin. Ceartas held piercing blue eyes and brightly colored blonde hair. The very air about him seemed to carry the Maker's presence in the man himself. She smiled slightly as she thought to herself, *being away so long from the Citadel, I wonder how devoted he truly is under that entire posh exterior?*

Her thoughts were interrupted. "Exactor Raven, please control your impulses. Do not think the contingent does not known how you look upon Ceartas. I would not want to have you succumb to your ribald desires just to be marked with the stigma of a sinner. Nor do we wish to have the righteous be tempted by the Defiler's temptress. Your duties are to purge yourself and sanctify yourself before the Maker," Purist Amháin quietly rebuked her as they came within earshot of the group.

Raven immediately composed herself in a more professional manner. "Understood, Purist Amháin, please forgive my roguish thoughts. I am but a simpleton in the Maker's great plan of Kuldarr. Your council and wisdom are, as always, a benefit and merciful in keeping servants such as myself on the path to righteousness," she replied.

"You may need much righteousness from the Maker in order to find this Master of the Order," the purist responded.

She was about to ask why when one of the other exactors next to Ceartas approached. "Ah! Raven, good to see that you will be assisting us with this small expedition." He extended his right hand in a Fermanian greeting, so she knew he was from the East.

Raven took the shorter man's hand and shook it. She had only seen and heard of him within the contingent but never really met him before.

"Trodaire Casein, right?" she responded. The muscular human in the platemail armor shook his head yes in acknowledgement. She saw that he had both a javelin and bastard sword strapped across his back. Raven found it a curious combination.

The other exactor moved forward and Trodaire turned his head in acknowledgement. "Of course you already know Dwyn Lani, our man of multiple other talents."

Dwyn was not dressed in platemail as the others, but in studded leather. The armor was gaudily decked out in bright hues of blue and the symbol of the Jasian Enclave. He was even shorter than Trodaire, by a few inches. He was very short for a man in general. He looked like he could weigh only eight or nine stone soaking wet, and that was with his armor. If he was abashed about his height, it didn't show in his confident posture.

Dwyn Lani wasn't a battler. As such, his armor and rapier were more for show. A representation of the might of the Jasian Enclave. He, like she, was more comfortable at range. So he sported a short bow on his back with a quiver of arrows. He also favored a bandolier with quite a few throwing knives. Raven envied him. She knew she could move far better with that type of armor but she had yet to prove her loyalty to the cause of the Maker. According to Amháin anyhow.

Unlike Trodaire, Dwyn was no stranger to her. They were long friends, since her first days in the contingent. She and Dwyn on occasion, when nobody was around, would sit and smoke some of the Spriggan's rare leaf and talk about their lives before their service to the Jasian Enclave. Both remembered what it was to be carefree and be on adventures to make a name for each other within the realm of Kuldarr. They both agreed that Amháin had it in for her. Raven was only one of two female exactors within Bray's contingent; all the other women were curates – healers. She, nor Dwyn could figure out the reason for his animosity towards her. Dwyn thought Amháin must not like women in general – and regarded her in particular as 'competition' to the adorations of men since the only other woman exactor was a spriggan; a creature that wasn't exactly comely in the eyes of humans or elves. Raven didn't really believe that Amháin favored men, but it was an amusing fiction to help them pass the time.

She nodded to Trodaire and acknowledged Dwyn. "Yes, we have consulted on many subjects of combat and survival skills we both have in common."

The trio of exactors was quickly interrupted by Amháin, "Good then. You will all have the basic resources you need to complete what is necessary by the Maker's will. Return the monk to the Order and restore the town of Agot. Additionally, eliminate any other threats left over from the previous attack. Wilders are to be offered no quarter, you are authorized to kill on sight, am I understood?"

Everyone nodded.

Ceartas added, "I would suggest we begin right away by getting over to the west side of town and determining what has happened to Master Ferric."

Raven nodded at that. "Agreed we must find these acquaintances and see what they can tell us."

Amháin looked in the direction they needed to go, "may the Maker bless you and protect you on this journey." He deftly moved past them and headed back into town. About halfway around the corner of the building by which they were standing, he turned back toward Raven. "Remember, Raven, do not stray from the path or you will be forever the Defiler's bitch," he declared and disappeared around the corner without a word to anyone else.

Dwyn smiled at Raven after the purist left. "Hells that man really doesn't like you."

"Guess not," she answered with a shrug of her shoulders.

Ceartas looked between the two. "Well he has a lot on his mind since Bray left. I know that is no excuse, Exactor Raven, for the way he has treated you for the last seven winters."

This was new twist in the purist, exactor rapport. Ceartas, though probably the most friendly to her of all the purists, never spoke to her favorably over his own people. Raven knew enough not to waste an opportunity that her and Dwyn long lulled over from many personal conversations. She placed her hand on her hip. "Do you know why he has been crass with me since I was assigned?"

"He has never liked the exactors. He believes that your caste will corrupt the Enclave in the long run. You being a woman in the contingent compounds the fears he has," Ceartas replied.

Dwyn chuckled and jabbed Raven in the ribs. "Guess a woman's place is in the healing tents, eh?" Dwyn skirted into the town quickly not waiting for a reply from Raven.

Trodaire gave a quick smirk at Raven and turned to Ceartas. "I am sure he was just joking. I don't think he meant any harm or disrespect toward the contingent's healing staff or to Raven."

The War-Curate placed his hand amiably on Trodaire's right shoulder. "Far be it from me to question the Maker's divine will on what and who he uses in the great scheme of things. Just because I have pledged my devotion to the Enclave doesn't mean I am no more a man than Dwyn." He let go of the shoulder then smiled toward the pair of exactors, "besides, even I have been injured many times and have found the women healers' skills very spiritually uplifting. They have a rather tender touch. In the name of the Maker of course. Now let's get on with this investigation."

Well all-be-damned, it appeared Ceartas was warming up to her after all this time together. Raven smiled at Trodaire then began moving into the town. The fighter just shook his head and followed after the group. "This is going to be one interesting investigation," he said to her as he jogged past Raven to catch up to the War-Curate and Dwyn. As she looked at the three walking before her entering the town square, she added under her breath, "Yes, this is going to be very interesting indeed."

# CHAPTER II

## 1

The town square of Agot was not as busy as it once was. The dry dirt paths in between the buildings and main area still bore the dark stains from the attack. An unpleasant reminder where the blood of many was shed. Daub and timber buildings were arranged in a square pattern around the town's large well. The area was approximately one hundred feet in any given direction from the watering hole. Raven saw this style often enough to know that, usually a few carts would be scattered between the well and buildings, selling various bits and baubles, or food stuffs. A square this size, and with the population Agot boasted, Raven could guess that anywhere from ten to twelve vendors might be spread out here at any given time of the day. Now though, there were only four. The group didn't need to be reminded why.

As the investigators made their way over to the eastern side of the square, Raven's eyes settled on the burnt remains of a single child's moccasin. There was no other to match it; it stood alone. Images of the woman collapsing into tears at the funeral only a scant hour before danced through Raven's green eyes.

She was barely aware that the half-collapsed building Ceartas led them to was once a bakery. Just outside a young man in his late teens was sweeping the front porch area, which felt futile with hollowed out carcasses of buildings that surrounded them. Raven saw that the right side of the building was folded in on itself, now exposed to the elements. Inside she saw directly into the living quarters of the baker and his family.

The shop itself was miraculously intact and boards were already in place to shore up and begin rebuilding the rest of the dwelling. A group of men, young and old, were hammering new pieces of wood up. Others were ripping off the worthless debris and placing it into the alley between the bakery and building next door.

The young man sweeping took notice of the group and stopped his task. Placing the broom at the door frame, he stated, "I am afraid we are done for the morning. You have missed the rush, what there was of it." He placed himself between them and the bakery.

Ceartas quickly replied, "That's fine young man, but we are here on a more investigative matter."

"Investigation?" he asked, looking back to the shop, confused. "Our damage was from the Wilders, not some vandals within our town."

Dwyn interjected, "We know. We are looking for someone that would visit your shop every once in a while."

The young man seemed to tense up, and his posture took a more surprised and shocked stance, as if he was to be questioned about some dark secret from long ago. He held up his hands passively infront of him, "Look, if this about Jaclyn, I can explain…"

Raven rolled her eyes, and sighed. *Jasians were infuriatingly conservative!* She pushed through the group of investigators and walked right up to the young man. He was startled and shifted like he wanted to run. Raven held up her hand to indicate he should stop. "Look, we are not concerned with your love life. We are looking for Master Ferric from the Order of the Sacred Fist. Our investigative team…" She gestured to the group now behind her. "– obviously has some information that indicates you may know him or of him, and who he visits on the west side of town."

"Ah you mean the guy in the white robe, dark-skinned, dark hair and eyes. Not from around these parts, maybe from Malten, or Gurgen. Lives in the monastery?" the young man asked.

Trodaire chuckled behind Raven, tried to cover it up with his fist like a cough.

Dwyn answered, "I think that would be him. You know – monastery – white robe – maybe some sandals – doesn't seem to carry any weapons. Kind of like a Master of the Sacred Fist. You do know that everyone that lives in that monastery is a monk, right?"

"Look we are busy every morning with lots of people and I don't pay attention to all that kind of stuff. We have orders to fill. All I know, he doesn't talk much. All I ever got out of him was he lives at the monastery and every two weeks he comes to pick up an order of breads, grains, and pies for one of the town's founders. He always overpays with three silver pieces," the young man replied, miffed at the group.

Ceartas moved up next to Raven's right. He smiled politely and gestured with open arms, "Look son, if you know the name of this founder it will help us locate Master Ferric faster. Then we can move along and let you get back to your more important business."

The young man placed his hand under his chin, tying to recall anything the investigators wanted. He ardently studied the ground in thought. "You said on the west side of town, right?"

"Yes," Raven replied

He looked up, taking his hand away from his chin and pointed at the group. "I think its founder Loach Hynafin, but I am not sure. You may need to speak with Norna Dewin, the grumpy old witch. She knows everything on that side of town."

"Did he say a witch?" Trodaire exclaimed from behind Raven and Ceartas. As he moved forward, Dwyn grabbed his right arm to halt him. Ceartas looked back toward the exactors and then back to the young man with a look of concern and determination. "I hope that she is not indeed a witch as you say, young man. Our contingent has been pursuing a sorceress in these parts for some time. If she is involved with Master Ferric's disappearance, things will turn very ugly, very quickly for this woman."

Raven placed her arm across Ceartas's chest, also slowing his advance. Gracefully she removed her helmet and cradled it against her hip. "I don't think she's really a witch. I think it's slang for the region," she said to the trio of men. Raven turned her attention to the young man, her eyes lit with fire. "I would suggest you explain your last statement, boy. I, being under the Jasian Enclave, am under obligation to eradicate all threats before they become a problem. The Enclave gives us a wide range of discretion."

The boy could only stare at her in confusion.

Raven sighed. "Let me put it to you this way – if the Jasian Enclave has evidence to prove any evil existed here in Agot, right now, they have full authority from the crown of High Province to purge this town. Substitute the Purists with the Wilders. All would be destroyed or sanctified which is equivalent to the same thing. Do you understand me? This town would be destroyed by the very authority of your queen."

The young man turned pale at the statement. His lower lip quivered as he tried to find the words. He took a deep breath, swallowed, and found his courage. "Norna is not a witch. All of us as children called her that. She is always crabby, and scolds everyone about not doing things the way she did them back in the day. She used to be an alchemist; word has it she still is. All she ever wants is to be left alone. It's just a rumor, you know? When anyone pulled a prank on her, when we was kids, the Mayor had a visit from Loach the very next day, and those responsible were caught and required to undo the wrong. We just called it magic, that she always knew it was us – that's all, honest to the Maker."

Raven lowered her arm off Ceartas and stared at the young man. Trodaire then spoke from behind, "This Loach sounds like a man of action." He moved closer to Raven. "Then why is a Monk of the Sacred Fist getting him food supplies every two weeks? If he is capable of coming into town to correct a wrong to someone, why can't he pick up basic needs?" Dwyn inquired now next to Ceartas.

Ceartas looked to the troop, "I guess we should go ask this so- called 'witch'," he said as he winked at Raven. He then brought his attention back to the young man. "We will get to the bottom of this, ser, by the Maker's will. I pray that what you have told us is true. If not, the Maker will have you reveal more to us if we return."

"It is, ser! I swear by the life of my mother and father! She is just an old crabby woman. Please don't purge me."

Raven turned to the group looking back and forth, "I think we have all we need here. There is no need to place more fear than necessary. These people have already suffered enough."

"Agreed," Ceartas answered. He waved to the young man to indicate he may go, "you have done a great service. We thank you."

The young man wasted no time, briskly abandoning the the investigators on the shop steps.

Dwyn stepped away from the troupe heading toward the west side of the square. "Well the day isn't getting any longer, people. Think it's time to see what else we can dig up on this Loach and Norna."

Ceartas followed, as did Raven and Trodaire. When Trodaire caught up to Raven he asked, "Do you think these two people have something to do with this monk's disappearance?"

Raven placed her helmet back on her head. "Not directly."

"How so?"

"I'll know more when we talk to these other two, if they are still alive, and I get a good look at the area," she said as she quickened her pace to match Ceartas and Dwyn.

Trodaire chuckled once more as he also matched pace with Raven. "So you're guessing right now?"

Raven smirked, "Let's just say I'm going with women's intuition."

"Oh, no. By the Maker, the last time you said that, things got real ugly and Amháin had no choice but to admit he was wrong in front of Aodhfin Bray!" Trodaire exclaimed.

"You were there for that?" Raven asked.

Trodaire nodded.

Dwyn interjected, "The ambush in the Spiral Drachen Pass on the way to Ethens in the Lugos Mountains."

"It was my first week," Trodaire remarked.

Ceartas whistled low. "If Raven is correct, we will adjust our tactics accordingly when the time comes."

"I got a bad feeling about this one, guys," Trodaire replied.

"I thought you were always up to a challenge, Trodaire?" Dwyn said, snickering.

Raven put her arm around the fighter's shoulders. "Let's not worry until we get more information, okay? I could be wrong you know."

The fighter laughed nervously. "Right and the skies are never blue."

Ceartas looked skyward. "They are not so blue when rain is near."

Full of mirth, Dwyn added, "There's some hope she's wrong then. You know the calm before the storm!"

Trodaire just shook his head as Raven let go of him.

# 2

The investigators walked a few blocks and slowly the full devastation of the Wilder attack unveiled itself like a morning fog rolling away.

Wattle and daub homes, their walls broken and windows rent, lined the dirt alleys in slightly curving rows. Fence of pliable hazel sticks wove between many such homes, shattered and splintered looking like the jagged maw of some feral beast. Blood stains adorned a great many openings, now dried ugly brown stains. These were a simple folk that died in the entrances of these homes defending loved ones, ruthlessly cut down by a superior foe.

Past those homes further into the western quarter, Raven could see that these houses were built with heavily fortified stone. This was the original Agot, before the gable-type houses were added on the east end of town.

Here the Wilder's desolation was thickest. Raven could see into almost every building to some capacity. Naked wooden posts were now all that separated the aisles within the homes, breaking up the living spaces. Doorways were smashed inward, while others were gutted by fire. Blackened char marks danced across everything and smeared window panes that somehow escaped the wrath.

A few homes were burnt completely to the ground. Blackened nubs and mounds of smoldering refuse all that remained of someones livelyhood. The very sight of it made Raven's core vibrate with rage.

When they entered a small clearing of shops they noticed a pub called, "The Drunken Priest". A half-broken door hung limply on its hinges, and boards were tacked up on the windows. Strangely, there was a bustle of activity inside.

"Good place as any to make some inquiries," Dwyn stated.

The quartet made their way to the damaged building. They could hear all the hustle and low murmur of the many patrons and staff before they even crossed the threshold of the doorway. The standard inquiries of the day's special – patrons asking for more ale, or reporting that the meal was satisfactory or not quite what the customer ordered. Typical tavern banter.

When they entered, the room fell silent except for the scrape of a chair or two within the hollowed space. The customers looked at the investigators nervously, as if they were waiting for another attack of some sort. It felt like time slowed to the speed of dripping molasses, but within a few moments, the customers began one by one picking up where they left off in their previous conversations.

Raven noted that some, however, were still watching the small group, suspicious of why they were truly there.

Ceartas moved forward towards the main bar where the owner of the establishment was hard at work. Dwyn, Raven, and Trodaire followed for a moment then made their way over to a table toward the back, nearest to the kitchen access. Upon taking their seats, Raven overheard one of the customers' low exchanges off to her left. She removed her helmet and placed it on the table. "I know, I know, Brackus, this attack was unprecedented. Now we have the Enclave here. What does it all mean?"

Raven glanced toward the table where the conversation was coming from. Among the empty wooden cups of ale were two plates of half eaten mutton, potatoes, and carrots. The two large gentlemen sitting took up most of the table themselves. They were dressed in the clothing of the land, possibly farmers or even simple peasants. Their grungy dark brown breeches adorned with various patches and small rips were complimented by their grey shirts, which also bore patches from their hard labor.

The man on the right began poking at his food and then slightly pointed toward Raven and the group with his fork before getting a potato, placing it in his mouth. She deduced that this was probably Brackus, for he was responding to his comrade's statement while chewing the food. "It means, old friend, that the way of the monks up at that monastery is no more. Look at 'em. Have you ever seen that type of Enclave soldier grouping, other than their leader over there talking to Reidwad?" He pointed to Ceartas at the counter with his fork, before taking his knife and cutting the mutton on his plate. The other man looked right at Raven and averted his eyes quickly. "No, but I think we need to finish and leave. That woman over there can hear us."

Brackus looked directly at Raven, staring with hazel eyes full of hatred. His long black hair was tied tightly around the back with a large braided ponytail that hung just over his right shoulder. "You have a problem, missy? Isn't any of your business, what we are talking about, so I'd suggest you mind your own, understood?"

Raven was about to make a snide remark when Ceartas came up to the table, diverting her attention from the man snapping at her. "Well that wasn't very helpful," the War-Curate stated. He looked at Raven, and the table where the men were, then back at her. "Did I interrupt something, Raven?"

Dwyn kicked back his chair on its back two legs and placed his feet on the table, crossing his arms behind his head, balancing himself. "In fact you did. I think Raven was about to teach that guy Brackus over there a lesson." Trodaire just pointed toward Raven and the stout man to their left at the other table.

"Why is that?" Ceartas asked.

There was a shifting of some chairs from the right of the War-Curate. A man was trying to calm his friend. "Brackus, no. It's not worth it," another voice from behind Ceartas called out. It was Reidwad, whom he had just talked to moments before. "Brackus, I just got this place presentable."

Ceartas turned to face Brackus, and he was confronted by a burly bear of a man standing half a head taller than him. As he looked up to the man he could feel the rancid breath upon his face and the heat of his body.

"Yes, why is that religious bitch going to teach me a lesson? She was eavesdropping on a conversation that was none of her business!" Brackus said with a spray of sour spittle in Ceartas' direction. The War-Curate easily avoided it by taking a step to his right, away from the table. He never took his eyes off the large man.

"Raven, how would you suggest we rectify this situation in a civil manner without endangering the innocent patrons of this fine establishment?" Ceartas asked as he stared intently into the other man's hazel eyes.

The attention of the two men was interrupted by the sound of armor clasps being undone from the table where the investigative team sat. When they both turned Raven was standing, and removing her armor's chest- and back-plate from her body.

Raven was proud of her figure, the hard tone of her well-muscled physique through winters of battle, hardship, and regimen, did not diminish her womanly assets. The combat bodice she was forced to wear to keeps such assets – restrained – only intensified her voluptuous, curvy figure that left most men a slavering mess.

While the men stared, she placed all her weapons on the floor. Next she put her left leg on the chair and began removing the armor from her dark green breeches. She noticed the hard leering from her leaning over position, and smirked slightly. "We take this outside gentlemen, so this…" She placed the one leg armor piece on the table and looked Brackus up and down then switched legs and started on the other buckles, "…angry little man can have his honor, or vengeance, restored as he sees fit. It doesn't matter to me."

Everyone in the establishment was in shock at the smaller woman disarming herself, getting ready to fight someone that had her by at least an arm's length and could pick her up and snap her like a twig. Trodaire looked at Raven with concern in his eyes. "You can't be serious?"

Dwyn, still in his comfortable position, snickered, "I am sure she will do fine. I'm just wondering how many blows before one of them falls."

Ceartas interjected, "Raven, this is… is… deplorable. You're supposed to represent the Jasian Enclave, and the Maker. How is this act righteous and of any aid to our mission?"

She placed the last piece of armor on the table and stared back at the War-Curate intently. "Did Amháin tell you the Maker requires your particular divine skill that allows you entrance into his presence and redemption of your transgressions for this investigation?"

"In not so many words he did, yes," Ceartas answered.

Raven made her way around the table and began moving to the main door. When in the doorway, she turned back toward everyone, "I am about to use my divine skill to get the information we need. Are you to question the Maker on how I am going to do this, or judge me because you're not as strong as you thought in his eyes?"

Ceartas sighed and grunted in frustration at the woman, "I personally do not approve of this, for the record."

Brackus shoved past the War-Curate. "Allow me to punish her for you, priest!" he moved toward the doorway. With a wicked grin, Raven turned out the door. As soon as she was gone, Brackus quickened his pace. Ceartas, Trodaire, and a few patrons moved from their positions to go outside to witness this event unfolding before them. Dwyn stayed behind, still in his chair, propped up. "Let me know if she knocks him down in five or less," he called out.

Raven was at the middle of the small street when she turned around to face the large man coming out of the inn. At the threshold of the door, she called out to him, "Okay farm boy, and let's see what's got your crotch all in a knot, shall we?"

Brackus exited the doorway along with about half a dozen of the patrons. Ceartas and Trodaire also were within the crowd as they dispersed along the porch on the front of the building. Everyone gave the big man a wide berth. Raven studied the event, but not the people. Instead she focused on all the debris scattered around from the repairs they had been making. She noticed a barrel on the right at the corner in front of the porch, a loose plank on the small awning over the porch above Brackus, and another right under the big man directly on the porch itself. She smiled and the large man saw it. Brackus pointed at her, his arm shaking furiously, "I'm going to teach you some manners, bitch!"

That was the only declaration she needed. Raven burst forward, her green eyes filled with determination and seething with righteous rage. She roared at him, "You're about to find out how much of a bitch I really am!"

Brackus braced himself for the little woman coming at him. He shifted his right leg back, crouching just enough with his left leg that he could grab her when she got in range.

Raven closed the gap like a bolt of lightning. Before making it on the porch itself she lept. Brackus smiled, knowing that she miscalculated and would land right into his grasp. Raven, in midflight, went forward into a somersault and positioned herself, landing with both feet on the loose plank on the porch, just beneath the monstrosity of a man.

Brackus, still smiling at his luck, grabbed her shoulders with his massive hands. White fire lit in his groin and flared up his body like a lit fuse exploding like a starburst in his vision. He had no choice but to loosen his grip, groaning in pain. Raven disappeared from his sight.

Trying to shake off the burn from below, he tracked the woman to his left, only to see her jump onto a barrel and then she vanished from his sight. Overhead he heard footfalls on the awning above. A shadow passed before him and she was back in front of him.

He shook the pain away and growled. Brackus lunged, only to see Raven quickly sidestep as a large plank that came from nowhere and hit him squarely on the center of his face. Again stars danced in his eyes and he was dazed. As he stumbled back he felt something like a noose around his neck and a body behind him on his shoulders. The pressure built, the stars ruptured into novas. He couldn't breathe! Then he heard the woman's small, senuous voice filled his ear, as Raven whispered gently, "When you wake up, farm boy, you better have some answers for us. I wasn't even trying. My preferred method would have been some bolts, an axe, and then my sword. The purist is the only person that is allowing you to live."

Brackus gasped for air. In a last ditch effort he backed up into the door frame to dislodge the woman. He heard a grunt from her, but her grasp only tightened. She whispered again, calm now replaced with anger, "Nice try, farm boy. Now you're my bitch. Good night!" Brackus fell to his knees his lungs screaming for air! He felt more pressure, and then pain in the right side of his neck and then he knew no more.

Raven dropped the large man onto the porch face-down. Everyone was in shock at what they saw. She brushed all the dirt and dust from herself. Turning to head back into the inn, Ceartas grabbed her arm with a look of muddled irritation, somewhere between fury at her, and concern for the man she just attacked. "By the Maker, if you just…"

She shook free of him. She tilted her head to him; defiant, and teasing. Her green eyes drank in the War-Curate, "your faith is the only thing that saved that man today, Ceartas. Consider it a gift for all your hard work. I would suggest when he wakes you get what information we need." She winked at him and stepped past the baffled man. As she entered the inn, Raven abruptly flipped her reddish brown hair with her hand as if nothing ever happened.

# 3

Trodaire approached Ceartas, looking down at the large man on the porch. "Did you know?"

"Know what?"

"That she could do all that?" the fighter replied.

Ceartas picked up the body to drag back into the inn. Trodaire assisted, and patrons moved in as well. Passing through the door into the inn, the owner, Reidwad, offered them a back room for whatever they needed.

They passed not far from their original table, where Raven was putting her armor back on. Dwyn was counting some coins and placing them in Raven's purse, obviously Raven took a rake for her victory. "Really? Not even one fist? You just used the building?" Dwyn asked in disbelief.

Raven looked up from her winnings directly to the healer and the fighter, seeing their concern. "Why so serious, guys? That was just to let off a little steam."

Ceartas looked at Trodaire, "I think I understand now why Amháin keeps a close eye on her. Did you see the way she looked at me back there?"

The fighter shifted his grip on the dead weight they were moving. "All I know, purist, is that I heard a rumor she was a Vadőr living in the Shemma at one time."

"A Vadőr? I thought they were more of a mountainous nomadic people. Nothing in common with a large forest or elves," the healer replied.

Trodaire shrugged his shoulders as they went past a hallway to an area where the rooms were, "it definitely explains how she was able to leap like that, and why she prefers ranged weapons."

They opened a door on the right to reveal a large room. Ceartas responded, "Still doesn't explain why she would have been in the Shemma. It does, however, explain how she knew about a possible attack in the mountain pass."

They entered the room with the bear of a man and placed him on a small bed. It took both of them to lift Brackus onto the bed. Dwyn and Raven entered, carrying buckets of water.

Raven was about to close the door when Brackus' friend stopped her. "Please don't hurt him. He really doesn't mean any harm." Raven grabbed the young man and pulled him into the room, shutting the door and locking it.

She turned to the group, looking right at the Ceartas and Trodaire. "Yes, I am from a Vadőr tribe. As for my business in the Shemma, that is no concern of yours."

"You heard that?" Trodaire asked.

Ceartas held up his hand to *stop*. The time for getting to know the group was not a priority, "we can talk about this later. Right now we need to pursue this lead Raven has provided."

Dwyn smiled. "May I?"

The War-Curate nodded to the exactor. Dwyn picked up a bucket and tossed the water onto the unconscious Brackus. The man immediately thrashed and moved his arms and legs about like he was having a nightmare. He ended up knocking over the bed and hitting the floor. Brackus stood up abruptly.

As that was happening Trodaire approached Raven, walking behind her to come around to her right side. He whispered near her ears, just under all the noise, "I'm curious what range, and if it's true what they say about Vadőr women – that they can be just as ferocious as the Wilder women."

Brackus turned to face the group before him, a dawn of understanding finally lighting his harsh features. Raven tilted her head toward the fighter and smirked at his words. "I am from the Impassable Range and you'll have to be a little more patient about my prowess in battle." She casually looked him up and down and added, "but at any time just say the word and I will be more than happy to spar in the practice area."

Raven moved up to Ceartas, still smiling.

Brackus saw his companion in the back. Bolstered, he immediately took a belligerent tone, "Justin, what the hells! We will be the first to disappear when these religious fanatics decide to purge Agot!"

Ceartas held up his hands passively, "look, Brackus was it? We are not here to purge anyone. We are here to investigate the disappearance of Master Ferric from the monastery. However, based on your behavior and hostile attitude toward us, I'm must question your motives, and on what you might know is going on within this town?"

Brackus smiled wickedly, folding his arms and leaning back against the wall. He harrumphed, "I know nothing, Jasian heretic. Go back to your walled city, where you judge others without fair council."

Just then another bucket of water assailed Brackus. It came from behind Ceartas and Raven. The big man frantically moved his arms and wiped the water from his head and hair. Ceartas turned back to the assailant. Dwyn slowly moved the bucket behind his back. "What? It slipped," the rogue stated in mock innocence.

The purist, frustrated with the situation, finally decided to regain his command. "That is enough!" he barked as he pointed to Dwyn. The War-Curate turned to Raven, still pointing, "by the Maker, you will contain your impulses properly to do this investigation with expediency, efficiency and without any more distress to the inhabitants of Agot. Do I make myself clear?"

There was movement near him and Ceartas felt the presence of the large man next to him eclipse him. The odor of wet dog blanketed Ceartas' senses.

Brackus chuckled sinisterly. "So let me get this straight, priest. You, being a devout man of the Maker, so self-controlled and ordered, cannot even contain those you command?" he crossed his arms again. "So these associates are – what –precisely? Exactors maybe? If the tales are true. They are nothing more than thugs used to beat and destroy that which your heretical doctrine deems unworthy."

Brackus looked each one of them in the eyes, "I think I am feeling distraught, being that I was attacked first, with no regard to my rights."

Ceartas let out a small breath of frustration and closed his eyes. He muttered a prayer to the Maker to give him strength for what he was going to do next. Opening his eyes he stared furiously at the big man, his blue eyes aflame with the determination of his faith. "Allow me to explain how this works, unsaved one. By the Maker's will, I will get to the bottom of this investigation. I do not care what you have against my church, my city, my people, or my god. Know this, however: as much as you think of me as a priest, I am a man of battle, forged by conflict. I have seen many such as yourself fall and fail to be claimed, by the defiler, or whatever other god, without proper forgiveness, calling out for their mothers at the end of their breath like weening children. Test me, Brackus. You instigated the fight whether due to your drunkenness, or just plain hate. It is clear you are in pain and that the pain has something to do with a woman or family you hold dear. If I am wrong, then you know something that has to do with Master Ferric or the founders of this town. Please give the Maker a reason for me to unleash his righteousness and justice where it needs to go, and not on a broken man mad at the circumstances he finds himself in."

Brackus looked the War-Curate up and down and could see Ceartas was primed for any conflict, his skillful, scarred hands, ready to un-hilt his gleaming silver mace. He even saw the capable brownish-red haired woman take a step away from the armored man before him. The other two were shielding his friend Justin of the coming violence. Everything hung on who would act first, or who would yield. Brackus impulsively asked the man before him a question. "Do you have a family, priest?"

"I do, a son, and a wife, but I haven't seen them in a long time," Ceartas replied, in a clipped tone.

Brackus backed up and picked up the bed. He set it upright, turned and sat down. "I did… as well, purist. Master Ferric tried to save them, but he was too late." When he looked back at Ceartas tears rimmed his red eyes. "I tried, but that wild woman… that wild man… last thing I saw was my dead wife and children. Master Ferric… I don't know what happened to him."

Tension bled from Ceartas. Relaxing he walked over to the broken man. He sat down next to him, leaned forward and folded his hands between his legs. "We will find him. We are heartbroken for your loss Brackus, but why instigate one of my own?" the War-Curate asked.

"Her eyes," Brackus growled.

Raven started to move forward, "My eyes… what the…?" She was halted by Ceartas with a gesture of his hand.

Brackus looked right at Raven, "You have the same wild look she had, that untamable look. Like there is an unbridled ferocity of chaos in you that can't be contained. Tell me, what is the difference between the Wildmen and the Enclave's thugs? Huh? You both want violence, you crave it," he replied with a tear running down the left side of his face. "I thought if I killed you it would make me feel better. I just wanted the green-eyed nightmare to go away. I needed to get rid of those damn eyes that will haunt me till my dying day."

Ceartas stood up and looked at Brackus, then toward his exactors. "Very well. Raven, Trodaire, I need you to leave the room, please. Dwyn, I need you to stay here with me and Justin while I converse with Brackus."

Dwyn was about to protest when the War-Curate held up his index finger. "Do as I instruct. If we are to find Master Ferric, by the Maker we need to heal this man's wounds properly." He nodded to Raven and Trodaire to go back to the common room.

And they obeyed.

# CHAPTER III

## 1

They entered the common room and one of the servants came directly up to them and immediately escorted them to a table. "Please, milord, milady…," a very young girl maybe ten winters in age said. "My father wishes to thank you for not killing Mr. Brackus. Your mid-meal is on the house for you and your group."

Raven smiled at the little girl as she took her seat. "Tell your father he is very welcome and we will welcome his generosity toward the Enclave."

Trodaire also sat and added, "yes, and we will have water with our meals, young miss. Thank you."

"No… no… thank you. My father has so much to do, and you prevented more damage that would set him back another month. I will go fetch your waters and bring your meals soon after," she replied. The two exactors nodded to the little girl, and she went off to get them their orders.

Trodaire focused back on Raven. "So, since we have some time, care to enlighten me on how you were in the Shemma?" he asked innocently.

Raven, her thoughts still on what Brackus had said about the Wildmen attack on his family, didn't hear the fighter's words. All she could think about was – *you have the same wild look she had, that untamable look. Like there is an unbridled ferocity of chaos in you that can't be contained.*

"Raven?" Trodaire asked, noticing her lack of attention.

She quickly shook her head, "I'm sorry. You were saying?"

He laughed. "I didn't think anything would faze you," the fighter stated. "I was asking if you were willing to tell me about the Shemma."

She sighed, but smiled when the little girl brought their water, and thanked her again. When the server left, she turned her chair and faced the fighter. "It was a long time ago, before I was with the Jasian Enclave."

"So you were there… interesting," Trodaire replied.

"How so?"

The fighter smiled. "I had a bet with some of the men in the contingent, when that rumor surfaced, that I could find out."

She laughed. "Really? How much was the pot when you were assigned to this task?"

"Thirty gold coins, at least half a winter's pay," he answered.

Raven turned her chair back toward the table, "I should have held out longer and negotiated a cut of the profits."

The fighter laughed. "Oh, so you knew about this. Why am I not surprised. Let me guess: woman's intuition right?"

She nodded. "Yep."

He turned his chair toward her as the food was brought to them and set on the table. He thanked the server and then put his attention back on Raven. "So a long time ago, before your service to the Jasian Enclave... I am curious why a Vadŏr from the Impassable Range would be so far from home?"

"It's complicated," Raven said as she picked up her wooden cup of water and took a sip. Trodaire could see the fire in her eyes as she said it. Obviously there was something more about this woman's past than her transgressions with a bunch of bandits or the Jasian Enclave. He looked at her for a moment, narrowing his right eye. He moved his chair back to position himself to consume his meal. "Fine... don't tell me. But I will just be a pest until we get this job done," Trodaire picked up his utensils and began to eat.

The two sat there, quietly eating their meal for a few moments. Raven had another refill of water from the server when she spoke, "I was captured by the slave traders of Malten after a skirmish against my mother's tribe. We were just north of the kingdom of Halsbren and I was a child of no more an age then our proprietor's young daughter."

"I take it you know who or what was responsible for that attack against your tribe?" Trodaire replied as he finished his mutton. He turned back toward her and took a sip from his cup.

"I do, and I would prefer to not proceed with this conversation," she said, turning her head and looking right at him. Her jade focus bore into his brown orbs.

The fighter turned back to the rest of his meal. "That's fine, Raven. If you could just answer me two things, I'll consider the matter closed."

"What's that?"

"How did you end up in the Shemma after the traders, and is it true that all Vadőr tribes are a society of women with no men?"

Raven smiled at the request. She took another bite of food and another drink of water. "There was a large storm that capsized the slave boat on the River Faith near the lake. I ended up near the Shemma, and was taken in by a Lefhym couple with small child who found me quite feral, near the forest. They were... keepers of knowledge. I learned all I could from them and enhanced my skills in the Shemma. I am what you call in some societies a – woodsman. Where I am from a - tracer. As for the Vadőr tribes, yes, we are a society ruled by women. Do we have men? Yes we do," she stopped and began to finish the rest of her meal.

Trodaire was about to say one more thing when she held up her hand, silencing him. He chuckled and finished his meal. In between his last few bites he retorted, "Wouldn't mind visiting one of those villages someday."

Raven placed her plate and cup off to the side, cleared her throat, and then folded her hands on the table. "Trodaire how can you have such an impure thought being one of the Enclave? What would Amháin do to you for such a thing? Oh, and by the way, our men have to earn their right to be by our side in all things." She looked at him, stand-offish. "So far you haven't impressed me."

He was about to answer when Ceartas approached and asked, "Is there anyone that has impressed you, Raven?"

Without missing a beat, Raven turned her head to the healer, and answered, "Ser Bray"

Dwyn piped in, "Him? Really, why is that?"

"His determination, magnetism, and the red within his hair are all the first qualities' Vadŏr women look for in their men," she replied.

Trodaire asked, "First qualities? There are more? And what is the deal about red in the hair?"

Raven sighed. "Red shows strength, fire of the mountain, and ferocity. Many Vadŏr women in leadership positions are red-headed. Many of our children are born with the trait, but by the rite of passage some fade to other colors, such as mine."

"So that's why..." the fighter began. But a look from Raven, ended his line of thought.

Dwyn spoke up, "Did we miss something?"

Raven changed the subject, "Ceartas, our meals are free for assisting with Brackus. Did you heal the man's wounds, as you put it?"

Ceartas and Dwyn sat down at the table and the little server girl came at once to give them their food and water. When the food was in front of them the healer said the blessing to the Maker. He then told them their next preparation in between bites and drinks of water. "Thanks to

Brackus, we have found out that Loach's place is not far from here. On the way we will be passing Norna's old shop she used to run. We should find some clues at either place. Justin also knew of a rumor that Master Ferric used to know Loach's father. According to both witnesses there was a group of four Wildmen attackers. One apparently was a woman warrior – which is rare. This group almost single-handedly did most of the damage we have been seeing in the area, and killed eight townsfolk. It would have been more if not for Master Ferric stepping in. They believe that he may have taken out two would-be assailants, and was pursuing the others."

"If that is the case he may be outside the town limits, and he's been gone a week, too? Only the Maker will know where he is at this point," Trodaire replied.

Raven looked at Ceartas. "Where is Brackus' dwelling from here?"

"About two blocks west."

Raven began to prep herself, making sure her armor was tightened. She double-checked her weapons then moved her chair and stood up. The rest of the group watched the woman secure her equipment as if she was going into battle. She looked at them, seeing that Ceartas and Dwyn were still in the middle of their meal, "I'd like to take Trodaire ahead to Brackus' dwelling if you don't mind. It may shed some light on what we may be facing."

Ceartas nodded as he was in the middle of chewing. Dwyn gulped down his water. "Hey, save some action for us," he said before cutting into his mutton.

The fighter secured his gear and briefly looked at Dwyn. "Don't worry, my friend. I am sure we will find nothing but debris." He walked past Raven and slapped her on the shoulder. "Shall we?" Raven shook her head in disbelief at his audacity, and followed.

# 2

After Raven and Trodaire left the inn they headed west, further into the town. Along the way they confirmed with a citizen the directions to Brackus' home to verify they were heading the right way. The two exactors' didn't speak. Their focus was on getting to their destination.

When they made it to the area in question, they could see the damage from the battle. There was debris everywhere, including planks in the street and shards of glass that had yet to be cleaned. Brackus' home was in shambles. The only thing that was left to identify it was the small family sign lying off what would have been the front porch stairs. The dwelling that was once a heavily-fortified stone and wooden rampart building now was a pile of burnt rubble.

Each home on either side was also damaged. It seemed that whatever hit Brackus' home hit all three at the same time. Trodaire whistled low. "Last time I saw damage like this it was done by a so-called sorcerer. Nasty work."

Raven sifted at the loose dirt all around, trying to find the imprints of any recent footfalls. Anything that resembled a walled-type depression. Moving slowly and methodically, she paced, sometimes in a circle at some particular spots. She checked the areas around the fronts of all the homes. She even went into a few of the devastated homes.

Townsfolk approached, curious about what she was doing, and unintentionally mucking up her scene. Raven motioned to Trodaire to intercept them so as not to disturb her investigating the grounds. She could tell over the past week there were many tracks that contaminated the area. She concentrated on the largest distortions. Raven separated between the many overall tracks with the potential true tracks she was looking for. She knew that if she read the area wrong, the actual targets her group was looking for, would be lost. During the investigation of the area, she noticed something strange. There were various scorch marks here and there which should have been nearer to the buildings. They were on the ground, like fire was thrown in different directions back at the suspected Wilders, not by the barbarians themselves.

She was well into her routine for a good fifteen minutes when Ceartas and Dwyn caught up to them. The healer and rogue could see that Trodaire was doing what he could to stave off the small crowd that gathered. Ceartas nodded to Dwyn to go assist the fighter. He then looked at the area, observing how close they were to the edge of the town now. Much closer to the farmland and foothills. He noticed that Raven was crouched down so he called out to her, "Anything interesting, Raven?"

She stood up and approached the War-Curate, and then whistled for the others. Trodaire and Dwyn left the townsfolk to allow them to go about their business. When they all gathered, Raven indicated for them to walk with her toward Brackus' dwelling. She spoke in a low tone, just above a whisper, "There were four in the beginning, just as Brackus and Justin said. One fell here." She pointed to an area off to their right, about ten feet away from the porch. "Two were in combat with our missing monk."

"And the fourth?" Ceartas asked.

Raven gave Trodaire a look, "Oh by the... I was right about something, wasn't I?" he stated.

She looked back to Ceartas. "Magic, and not ours, was used here."

"Ambrosia?" Dwyn asked.

The War-Curate's face grew dark with concern. "It fits the description. A female with Wildmen, wild eyes, and now magic. We may have to get the rest of the contingent and inform Purist Amháin."

"No...there's something else," Raven interjected. "Besides the strange fire strikes at the Wilders on the grounds here."

"What?" Trodaire asked.

Raven pointed over to where the one Wildman had fallen. "There was a set of small snake-type tracks that burrowed into the ground. I have seen snake holes, but never like this or with that type of tunneling."

Dwyn grimaced. "Small snakes that burrow into solid ground? I thought they were bigger and in certain areas, not around here."

"Ceartas, which way is the alchemist's and founder's dwellings?" Raven asked.

The War-Curate pointed to the southwest. "It's about another block over. Maybe five or six buildings that way. Why?"

Raven looked in that direction and then toward the empty space of the farm and hilly area more to the west. She relied on her training from her adopted brethren, the Elves. "There were also two other pairs of footprints, not belonging to Wilders. One seemed to be limited, almost lame. You can tell by the slight scraping of the ground. What is strange about it is that the tracks moved in a pattern of a normal faster-paced individual with no injury to support the wound. Many with that type of wound, the scraping would be at least two to three times larger. The other was small strides with faint depressions, maybe an Elf could make these but I have not seen any other Elves in town, though that's not to say they aren't here. The logical conclusion would be a tiny woman or a child. Both seemed to have engaged the Wildmen along with the monk. They retreated back toward the direction you indicated, with a single Wilder giving chase. Two Wildmen took off running due west, with the monk in pursuit.

Dwyn looked at Raven. "Why would a Wildman not engage the bigger threat of Master Ferric, but instead go after the two others? It isn't their style or tactics."

Snapping her finger, Raven exclaimed, "The alchemist shop!"

Ceartas looked at the woman. "We have one of two possibilities. One, it's Ambrosia going to go get components to keep her power over the Wildmen; or two, one of her trusted fighters went to get the components for her."

Trodaire added, "Begging your pardon, Ser, but an alchemist doesn't have magic. They deal in chemical compositions with solids and liquids."

"No, they also carry magical components to enhance those items. I also know some may have limited spell creation just as so-called Creationists," Dwyn answered.

Ceartas looked at the members of his team individually. "We need to find out what has been taken from that shop. This way we have an idea of what to expect from our enemies when we go to engage them. Let's move exactors. Time is already against us."

# 3

They ran down the street, then turned right and moved west to the next block over. When they came to the shop of the alchemist, Norna Dewin, it was oddly intact with little sign of damage. Ceartas stopped short and held his group back with a move of his arms on either side of him. "This isn't right. Do we have the right place?"

Dwyn pointed up by the awning on the porch. "Yep. There is the sign." The notice was in an oak frame with hickory back, which was painted in white markings — Dewin's Spiritual Concoctions and Goods.

"Raven, tracks, I want to know who came here and where they've gone. Dwyn, I need you to go check up there cautiously, and then make your way toward the back. I don't like this," Ceartas commanded.

The rogue smiled and almost skipped as he moved forward. "On it boss. I'll make sure we don't trip anything as small as a spider web." He slowed when he was near the porch. About ten feet out he searched where he was safe to step.

"Trodaire, I want you to go over to the building to the right, and from behind make your way to the back with Dwyn. Understood?" the War-Curate ordered. The fighter nodded.

Ceartas whispered a small prayer for victory and protection for his exactors and moved forward toward the small shop. As he was about halfway to his destination, Dwyn gave a thumbs-up for the area then pointed to the door and indicated it had some possible damage. The rogue began his journey to the back, going to the opposite side of the building Trodaire did.

Ceartas made it to the bottom of the stairs, stopped, and closed his eyes. "Exactor Raven, I need an assessment please."

Raven walked up next to him and whispered in his right ear, "All three tracks lead here. The tracks indicate the small one first, then the lame one, lastly the Wildman. All of them entered from this direction. No exit tracks at all, unless they left out the back." She looked around quickly to see if anyone was watching them. "All is clear so far out here. Should I cover you at range?"

Ceartas seemed to be in some form of meditation, taking Raven's words in. He opened his eyes. "No. Prepare for CQB. I don't want anyone to even have the opportunity to escape this dwelling. Understood?"

Raven nodded. "Shall we?" she asked as she untied her throwing axe for easy access.

The two warriors slowly went up the small stairs, hands on their weapons as they approached the door. They immediately noticed that it had once been off its hinges but was very recently repaired. Ceartas was about to try the door handle when they heard a "psst..." from their right. They looked and it was Dwyn. He whispered to them, "All clear, nothing but a bunch of smelly, dead-stinking trash with glass, wood, and things I don't recognize."

Ceartas nodded, and using hand signals instructed, "sneak in the back." Dwyn nodded and disappeared back around the corner. The War-Curate focused on the door handle and found it unlocked. He and Raven opened the door and entered.

A small bell over the door rang as they entered. They heard a young voice call from the back of the four large, shelved isles of bottles, "Afternoon. Please... please... come in, come in. What can old Norna or I do for you?"

Cautiously, Ceartas and Raven moved forward, still with their hands on their weapons. The War-Curate was concentrating on the young woman at the counter. Raven happened to glance at the shelving and noticed it was all new construction and stocked with new bottles. She coughed to get Ceartas' attention. When he looked she nodded to the shelves. He returned the nod and pressed forward.

The shop had various jars and bottles filled with many differently colored liquids and substances and items such as fingernails, and bear's claws. Raven even thought she saw the eyeballs of some type of animal. The place smelled like fresh vanilla with hints of lilac.

As they closed in on the counter they could see a young woman in a grey and blue flower-patterned sun dress. She had a small leather belt with a pouch. Her back was to them while she stood on a stool putting away a few jars on a large shelving cabinet behind the counter. Her amber hair glistened in the sunlight provided by the four windows of the shop. She came down off the stool and turned around to face the duo. Her large brown eyes sparkled with happiness. She couldn't be more than about twenty-winters-old. She was small-framed but average in figure. She reached over to her pouch and pulled out a small flask, then took a sip and put it back. She asked them, "how can I help you today?"

Ceartas, still holding his hand on his weapon replied, "We would like to talk to Norna, please. It's about Ser Hynafin."

The girl's eyes widened. "Oh, my, has he run out of his medicine again?"

"Med...," Ceartas was about to ask, when Raven grabbed his arm and interrupted, "Yes, seems he is going through a lot of it due to the recent attack."

"I see. Well let me get the extra Norna made for him," she said as she moved behind the counter towards the back. She disappeared into a storage area through a small doorway. As soon as she was out of view Raven and Ceartas heard the footfalls of someone running. They immediately realized it was the young girl, they gave chase. Seconds after entering the back room, they could hear her yelling, "No... no!"

Past rows of shelving, in an open area, was a huge table with a large fabric tarp on top of something. On the other side, just beyond it, was the rear door. The woman was held there by Dwyn and Trodaire. The fighter smiled as he escorted the woman back in to the apothecary. "Lose something, Ceartas?" Trodaire pushed her forward toward the War-Curate.

Raven noticed that the area was highly scented with various candles, incense, oils, and assortments of dried petals and spices in various bowls and urns spread out all over. She took a deep breath through her nose and found another fragrance; carrion and rot.

"I didn't do anything! Let me go!" the young woman yelled.

Ceartas looked at her intently. "Then why did you run?"

Raven slowly moved toward the table as the group at the other end questioned the girl. The odor was definitely stronger there. Out of the corner of her eye she glanced dried blood stains on the floor and on the bottom of the tarp.

"I was told by Norna if anyone came looking for Ser Hynafin I was to go to his home and wait until she returned," the frightened woman replied.

Raven saw a large protrusion off on the right side, like something was holding the tarp off the table. She slowly approached it and studied it more closely.

Trodaire interjected, "Why would she have you go there?"

The woman looking at the group saw Raven getting closer to the tarp on the table. She frantically answered, "She said it would be the only place I would be safe..." Raven was beginning to reach down to the side of the tarp. "No! Don't touch that!" the woman cried out.

Raven pulled back the piece and saw a large hand in the rictus of a claw. She immediately grabbed the rest of the tarp and ripped it off the table. The young woman screamed out, "No! You will release the plague!" and tried to free herself from the fighter.

On the table was a Wildman in a slow state of decomposition. His legs were gone, sawed off in order to fit him on the table. Raven guessed he would have been about seven feet tall. All he had on him was some skins and furs, virtually no armor. His chest was exploded open, the breast plate broken in half, exposing internal organs. Dwyn moved off to the side and threw up his lunch next to the back door. Trodaire loosened his grip on the woman, but quickly held fast as she began to writhe. Ceartas had nothing to say but, "By the Maker..."

Raven briskly moved around the table towards the captive woman. She pointed to the body. "What happened here?"

"You have to cover the body or the plague will be released!" she cried wildly.

"A cover on a body does not prevent a plague," Raven answered.

She shakily started to point toward the shelf next to the table. "But the creatures will come and take us over."

Raven's eyes followed the direction over to the shelf in question. Ceartas moved over toward the young woman. "Who is this Wildman?" he demanded.

"He was the shaman. He destroyed Brackus' home with fire from his hands. That's what Norna said," the woman answered.

Dwyn, recovering from his slight sickness, said, "Wildmen don't use magic; they hate it."

Trodaire released the woman to Ceartas. "Yet they follow Ambrosia, who is a sorceress."

Raven, moved over to the shelf. It contained various labeled elixirs and salves for many things: health, rejuvenation, and – one that she recognized for another purpose. She quickly checked if the others were paying attention – especially Dwyn. They were so involved with the woman they were not looking at Raven. She plucked the small bottle form the shelf, ripped off the label, and placed it in her traveling pouch. When she looked up she saw something she had never seen before. The creature in the large jar was about twelve inches in length and just bigger in diameter than an arrow shaft. She could see a trisecting jawed mouth, frozen in mid-opening. She could also see what looked like undeveloped wings fused on the side of its body. It had the characteristics of a small snake. She picked up the jar and faced the group with it.

"It's quite dead, but I have never seen anything like it." She handed it over to Trodaire.

He looked at it then handed it to Dwyn. "What is it" he asked, looking back at the woman.

Dwyn shook as a shiver passed through his body, and then put the jar on the table next to the corpse, "that came out of him?"

The woman quickly answered, "He followed Norna and Ser Hynafin here to the shop. I was in the back when everything was being destroyed. Norna managed to subdue him with one of her gaseous elixirs, and Ser Hynafin cut him down. It was when they brought him back here…" she pointed to the jar, "…that thing came out of his chest and made a Maker awful noise. I couldn't move, nor could Hynafin. Norna was the only one that could move because she is mostly deaf. She took one look at it, grabbed her dagger and sliced it in half then placed it in the jar. After that we did our best to clean the shop up all week, but she wanted to study the Wildman. When she heard that Master Ferric was missing, she told me to stay here and trust no one. If anyone came asking for her or Ser Hynafin I was to go to his place until she returned and she knew it was safe."

Ceartas placed his hand on his forehead and rubbed his brow. "So let me get this straight. A deaf woman, and a lame but capable fighter show up to fight Three Wilders, one being a woman, who were already engaged with the monk. Things go bad and two leave with the Monk in pursuit while this one…" the healer pointed to the dead body, "…has magical powers and goes after the deaf and lame targets only to be taken out by them, and is infected by some worm or snake creature? Then when the rumor surfaces that the monk is missing, these same two individuals go to save Master Ferric?" He looked at the woman. "Young lady, I think there is more about your employer than you're telling us. I would suggest you come clean. I am not about to have my people engage this wild woman who may be a powerful sorceress."

The woman began to cry. "How do I know I can trust you? Norna said I could only trust her."

Raven walked up to Ceartas and placed her hand on his shoulder. "Let me handle this," she said quietly.

Ceartas nodded and then turned to the others. "Let's get this poor bastard out of here and give him a proper burial. I am sure the rest of him is outside in that garbage." Trodaire and Dwyn nodded and opened the back door and then went to get the body moved while the healer began a prayer ritual.

Dwyn spoke up, "Ceartas, can you extract the final thoughts of those that have passed?"

The War-Curate nodded while not breaking the chant.

Trodaire grabbed one end of the body while Dwyn had the other. The fighter added, "That's what he's going to do while we bury this guy, so we can get more information." They moved the body out the door of the shop.

When the men left, Raven led the young lady by the hand and took her back to the front of the store. "We are not here to harm you, Norna, or Ser Hynafin. We are investigating the disappearance of Master Ferric. Any information you have that can help us understand why he has not returned or why there is a relationship with Norna and Hynafin would be of great help. The Order needs him back soon. They are lost without his guidance. Do you understand?"

The young woman nodded.

Once in the front of the store, Raven placed the young woman back behind the counter and she took a seat on one of the stools opposite her. She folded her hands in front of her and asked, "How about you tell me what happened here when that Wilder showed up?"

The young lady took a deep breath, closed her eyes and then looked at Raven. "I was in the back gathering all the healing agents I could for the town, when I heard Norna and Hynafin come running in. It couldn't have been more than a few seconds later when a crash echoed after them. That was the front door coming off the hinges and smashing into the first shelf," she explained. "I slowly moved to the front when I heard the Wildman scream at Norna."

"Like a spell or something?" Raven commented.

The woman shook her head. "No he was very clear. He said something about he thought she was dead hundreds of winters ago and she would not escape him, now. When I looked around the corner Norna threw three bottles, and a cloud formed and engulfed the Wildman. When the smoke cleared, the attacker was frozen in place and Hynafin ran his sword through his chest, killing him."

Raven blinked at the woman in surprise, "what did he mean by her being so old, and how is that related to Ser Hynafin and Master Ferric?"

The young woman reached over and grabbed her flask and took another drink from it. When she put it back she looked at Raven. "She knows a lot of old history, but has no books here about it. Norna also knows things about components and elixirs that can extend one's life."

"So what, you're older than you look?" Raven inquired.

"I am forty-one winters old," the young woman answered. She didn't look a day over twenty.

Raven looked around the shop. "So some of the things I have seen here are what Dwyn told us. It's a store with a gathering of many different things that also have magical properties." She slowly reached down without the young woman noticing and tapped the pouch that had the vial she grabbed earlier.

The woman nodded, "I am Norna's apprentice, Maggie."

"Pleased to meet you Maggie. So what is the connection between Hynafin and Ferric then?"

"The founder was on an adventure with his father and Master Ferric many winters ago when he was wounded with a crippling injury, never to walk again. Ser Hynafin's father was killed shortly after, but before his demise he made Master Ferric promise to keep an eye on Hynafin from a distance," Maggie replied.

Raven stood up. "So what exactly? They made it here to Agot when it was just a hamlet and met Norna?"

Maggie nodded. "She gave him medicine to help him walk again, but over the winters it has been wearing off more and more quickly. Master Ferric joined the Order at the monastery soon after and over the winters became one of the masters. It's taken about twenty winters, but Agot has grown to what we have today thanks to our exclusive trade deal with the dwarves of Ethens."

"Thank you, Maggie. You have been helpful. Now we just have to find out where they went to assist Master Ferric," Raven said. She stood and started to make her way toward the back door to the others.

Ceartas met her in the doorway and stopped her. "Norna thinks Master Ferric is in danger and will not survive the other two Wildmen."

Raven just blinked at the healer. "Why do you think that?"

"During the extraction of information from the dead Wilder, I found that he was not in control of himself." Ceartas seemed shaken. "Apparently he knew things of an ancient nature and Norna is not what she seems. She assisted another person, a woman named Shanti centuries past, which this entity, or demon, hated."

"Are you alright?" Raven asked concerned.

Ceartas composed himself and looked at Raven with a divine determination, "I am worried for Ser Bray, It's public knowledge in the Citadel that Bray had a decendant named Shanti. I pray that the Maker will protect him out there in the Wilds.

"We, however, need to go assist Norna and Hynafin. Luckily the Wilder here was the only magic they had. However, if there are more of those snake demons I fear for all who engage those Wildmen. This whole thing could be a trap for all we know. It will take too long to gather the contingent. We must move with haste for I fear we may be already too late for Master Ferric."

Raven walked up to him and placed her hand on his shoulder. "I have an idea which direction they went. I can find them," her voice confident.

The two moved out the back of the store toward the other exactors. They were just finishing up covering the grave they made for the Wildman. When they approached Dwyn asked, "So I take it we are off to find this vagabond group?"

Ceartas just nodded. Trodaire picked up the shovels and began to walk back where they borrowed them from. "Be right back, don't start without me," he said smiling.

Raven could see the concern on Ceartas' face. The man seemed deeply troubled about the events that transpired within Agot. She again tried to reassure him, "This won't take long, trust me. I have a good idea where to start tracking."

Dwyn, seeing Trodaire returning, said, "Well, guess you should begin. We only have about seven hours before it gets dark and you lose the trail."

As the fighter rejoined the group, Raven looked at the leather-bound companion and smirked. "Just because it gets dark doesn't mean I still can't track."

Ceartas took a deep breath, and then said a small prayer. Once done he looked at his comrades. "Very well, let us be off. It's time to find this monk of the Sacred Fist and return him to where he belongs." The group nodded and began their journey back toward Brackus' house to pick up the trail of their adversaries.

# 4

It didn't take long. Within the hour the group was heading out into the Agontill Highlands. The rolling grassy hills consisted of rich plant life with large areas of small wetlands and vibrant verge towards the steppes of the Impassable Range not far in the distance. The foothills were drained by small creek beds that filtered to Agot and further into the Wilds. They also contained outlying disconnected areas, such as valleys, where many farmers were cultivating the lands and herding animals.

Raven was grateful for the moderate climate of the region. It reminded her of her home, which was so close now she could almost touch it. She admired the various pleasant woodlands here and there, especially towards the mountains – towards home.

As tracker, Raven was at point, leading the men by a good hundred paces or so. Dwyn was much closer to her, acting as overwatch with his bow, following only fifty paces behind her. The two were long practiced in this method, and Raven felt comfortable knowing Dwyn had her back.

She continued to survey the terrain all around her. The tall grass, the small dirt paths, trying to find any recent footfalls that would have created the typical walled-type depression that indicated a foot print. Wilders prints should be easy to find, as large and heavy as they were, but she was also trying to find Master Ferric's footfalls. Much lighter it made the trek a ponderous affair. They only rested twice, taking in food rations or drinks of water. After four hours in the foothills, Raven noticed that the tracks turned toward the south – towards the Wilds. It was here that Master Ferric's rescuers prints were now added in to the mix.

A unique whistle pierced the silence. It resembled a small bird trilling. She knew Dwyn's call. Raven looked back and saw the rogue pointing ahead of her and up toward the sky. When she looked to the direction he indicated, she found scavenger birds circling in the empyrean heavens. She turned back to the thief and nodded, then continued forward.

It still took another two hours before Raven crested the rise of a hill and saw the slaughter below. She immediately dropped into the tall grass. The tracker indicated to Dwyn with a quick wave of her arm behind her that there was danger up ahead. He dropped to a crouching position and gave the bird call back to the others. They drew their weapons and crouched down as well.

Raven figured that in the six hours they had easily traversed at least twelve miles west to southwest of Agot. The exactors, as always, were efficient. She'd hoped to make it in a single day, but she hadn't been sure. It looked like their luck held. Slowly she lifted her head, using the grass to conceal her, she took in the scene below.

A stone cottage with a thatch roof was below, and still largely intact. There was a wooden barn off to the left that was also unharmed. What was disturbing was that all of the animals from the barn were all slaughtered in the open area outside, including the inhabitants of the small plot of land. Off to the right was a third stone building and another set of bodies. Scavenger birds were all about, picking and fighting amongst themselves for any piece of the carcasses they could bite into. Raven about jumped up when she heard Dwyn whisper next to her, "What is that over by the stone building, a large lizard?" *By the gods that man could be quiet!*

Raven easily saw what he was refering to. "I'm not sure from this distance, but it kind of looks like a drachen, what I would guess you now call a dragon, in civilized areas," Raven whispered quietly.

"Dragon! Holy hells, I didn't think I'd ever see one in person. I don't see its head. Matter of fact, I don't see any heads on any of those corpses," Dwyn answered, his voice growing tense.

Raven could hear the other companions approaching from behind. They were about a good ten feet from her and Dwyn when Ceartas whispered loudly, "What do you have?"

Raven slowly moved away from the edge of the hill to converse with the team. Dwyn followed soon after so as not to give away their position. As she approached she quickly glanced behind her to make sure Dwyn was not far. She looked at Ceartas. "The tracks lead down to a farm. Everything is dead down there, based on what I can see from here. I won't know any more until I get down there. I don't know if the Wilders or the monk is still there."

Dwyn spoke up while taking Raven's left side. "Raven thinks there is a possible dead dragon down there as well, guys! I think that bad feeling you had, Trodaire, is about to come into play."

Ceartas' brow darkened at the sound of that. "A dragon? No one has seen a dragon in centuries. Are you certain?"

Raven quickly replied, "I'm not sure, but based on my studies back in the Shemma with my foster family, it looks like it may be. By the look of it from this distance it's huge, about fifteen feet long. I've never seen a lizard so large."

Trodaire's face grew discouraged for a moment, and then he took a deep breath. When he composed himself he said, "A lot of horrible creatures live in the Wilds. Maybe this big nasty wandered out. The only way we are going to find out what it is, is to get down there.

"I don't like the fact that these Wildmen can take out something that large. If that is the case, what hope do we have for Master Ferric?"

Raven looked at the group. "Maybe none." Her honestly, clearly didn't encourage the men, so she continued, "Either way we have to find out. Maybe he escaped when the large lizard showed up." She looked at the healer. "So what's the plan?"

"Is there any other way down to the farm than this hill?" Ceartas asked.

Raven pointed to his left. "If you go that way you can go down and re-approach as if coming from a path to the farm."

The healer nodded. "Okay, Trodaire and I will take that route and draw anyone watching the main path to us." He looked at Raven, tilting his head to the right, "is there another path that way?"

Raven nodded. "Yes, it will come up behind the storage building."

"Dwyn, you go the opposite side of us and see if you can approach from that building to the main house." Dwyn saluted and moved to start his portion of the plan.

The healer looked back at Raven. "You position yourself up here with range and provide cover fire. Hit anyone that attacks us. Understood?" he commanded.

Raven nodded again, and slowly moved back to her original position at the top of the hill. She crunched down and hid within the tall grass. Ceartas and Trodaire moved off.

Raven slowly removed her repeating crossbow from her back and began looking for a better vantage. The tall grass was good cover but not close enough range for what she wanted to do. She scanned the area and found a few large boulders imbedded into the hillside toward the farm. She looked for the least possible way to be seen to each of the three hulking stones she could use.

The crawl to the first boulder was about twenty-five feet down from the top of the hill. She risked a quick look to the trail. She could see Ceartas and Trodaire just coming around the bend toward the barn. She then glimpsed back to the storage building, and still didn't see Dwyn, though that hardly surprised her. She probably wouldn't see him until the action started.

Raven went low again and started crawling toward the second boulder, now about halfway down the hill. When she reached it she got up with her back against it and swiftly peeked around the cover for another look at where her team was.

She saw the healer and the fighter amongst the dead carcasses, chasing away the birds, looking for survivors. They were maintaining constant vigilance toward the house should anyone come at them.

Only by sheer luck Raven, caught a glimpse of Dwyn behind the main house in the back. He waited until she made eye contact, and he gave her a thumbs up and darted toward the house.

Raven, for the third time, crouched down and moved to her final destination of the third rock formation, bringing her less than thirty feet from the base of the tall hill. Once there she positioned herself behind the natural cover and found a niche from which she could fire on any opponent. No sooner did she hunker down, when all hell broke loose.

There was commotion from within the house, and a scream that sounded like a battle cry. Next thing everyone heard was crashing and several thuds throughout the home.

Glass exploded outward of the front of the homestead, glittering like clinquant diamonds in the dying light. Amidst the crystalline slivers, Raven spied a body. It barely cleared through one of the main windows of the stone structure. The person did a forward tuck and rolled in a somersault. Momentum was not their ally however, and he continued to roll kicking up dirt and dust before lying prone on his back. It was Dwyn. Several puckering wounds oozed the life from his chest.

Ceartas and Trodaire immediately moved to his side. The fighter took a defensive position with his sword out and the curate tried his best to begin healing the man on the ground.

Two Wilders exited the home in frenzy. One was seven feet tall and had to be no less than three feet wide. Saber-tooth tiger skulls adorned his hands and a basilisk's skull was on his head. The hardened muscles of his arms were holding a massive axe. His bare chest was covered in blood still streaming from up by his neck. The second one was seven-and-a-half-feet tall and three-and-a-half-feet wide, and definitely a female. She was sporting leather and fur that covered her large muscular frame and minute bosoms in a battle bodice of reinforced snakeskin. Her shoulders each had basilisks' skulls on both sides. On her head, fresh still with pockets of scales on the skull, was the horned frame of a lizard. This Wilder also had bone-plated legs and forearms with saber-tooth skulls on both hands. She held two axes without effort.

The smaller of the two Wildmen ran up toward Trodaire. So close the human fighter looked like a child next to the giant man. The Wilder swung his axe with brutal efficiency. Trodaire was put purely on defense, parrying every blow in an effort just to survive. Raven watched as each impact weakened the fighter's arms against the mighty strength of the larger man.

She had no shot! Trodaire kept weaving into her line of fire every time he parried. "Dammit Trodaire move out of the way!" she hissed.

Raven looked to the other opponent. The Wilder woman just watched, licking her lips and waiting for something. She could shoot her and be done with it, she should shoot her, but something stayed her hand from aiming at the large woman just yet. If she did, and the Wilder dispatched Trodaire, he could kill Ceartas and Dwyn before she could line up another shot. No – she needed to wait for a clean shot unless the big woman made a move.

Another blow sent the fighter off to one side, exposing his left flank. The Wilder countered again and sliced deep into Trodaire. Raven concentrated, focused her sight and steadied her aim. As Trodaire collapsed on his knees to the ground, the Wilder spun around to cleave the head off the fighter. Raven exhaled and squeezed the trigger.

Five bolts found themselves directly center mass of the Wildman. Raven knew even that dense body couldn't prevent her deadly bolts from piercing his heart. The warrior stumbled back in shock, bewildered as he looked down at the feathery protrusions. He fell to the ground dead his last heartbeat later. Raven quickly reached behind her into her pack and grabbed another magazine of bolts. She hit the quick release on the crossbow, dropping the empty one.

The surviving Wilder screamed a battle cry enraged at the loss of her companion. Drool and foam cascaded from her mouth from under the hideous skull. Her green eyes were aflame with hatred at what just transpired. She leaped from the doorway, swinging both axes in a forward motion like a saw about to cut wood.

She was running right at Trodaire to mow him down. Her speed was impressive. Raven was trying to reconnect the magazine to fire again but knew that she would not get it in time to save the fighter. "Sorry Trodaire," she whispered.

A loud clash of metal echoed in the valley just as Raven connected the cartridge in its place. She immediately repositioned herself in a firing stance in time to see Ceartas knocking the woman off her target with a bash of his shield. This just infuriated the Wild woman more. She swung, and Ceartas deflected again, causing her to miss the still-kneeling Trodaire only by inches with her axe head.

Raven took aim as the woman spun around to engage the War-Curate. She was about to do another center mass when Ceartas got in the way. "Damn it!"

Her eyes fell to Dwyn, he lie deathly still. Trodaire looked to fair little better on his knees, blood hemmoraging horribly out his side. The only thing standing between their life and death was Ceartas, and he was only a single mistake away from doom himself, facing this superior opponent. She had no choice. Raven had to take the shot. Against all rational judgement and training, she re-adjusted to account for her target's cover, Ceartas, she took a deep breath, held it, counted to three, and fired.

Ceartas came up quickly to put distance between him and Trodaire from the wild woman. He placed his shield between the two of them to guard him against the woman. He was taking his battle mace and swinging from the right when he felt the pull of five wisps of air rip by him. The sound followed half a breath later.

He connected with the mace into the woman's lower jaw, knocking her back and giving him momentary respite. Then he saw the bolts. One in her upper right thigh, one in each of her shoulders, the fourth in her left upper thigh, and the Wild Woman was no longer wearing her dragon skull!

She was a terror to behold. Perhaps more frightening without the helmet than with. Her braided hair, matted in caked blood, came tightly to her wide forehead. Her entire face was decorated in multiple inky black tribal tattoos. Those fierce green eyes that Brackus was haunted by, were enhanced with the thick blackened outlines of her fearsome tattoos. Ceartas was certain that the Defiler himself was in possession of this gargantuan beast of a woman.

Unfazed by the pain of the wounds in her body, the Wilder seemed to be re-assessing her position. She casually glanced at the fletching protruding from her body like feathered fingers.

She then let go of her axes and let them drop to the leather straps tied to her wrists. She charged Ceartas. He braced himself for the impact.

Raven saw the woman run up and instead of bashing the War-Curate, she grabbed his entire body, shield and all. The Vadőr woman knew he would not last long. She quickly studied the area, noticing any footing that would give her the high ground, and reloaded her final bolt cartridge into her crossbow, loosening her armor straps. An idea came to her and she hesitated only a moment before she reached into the pouch that contained the vial she took from the alchemist's shop. She opened the bottle and pulled her longsword. Raven swiftly added a few drops of the substance onto the blade, and then re-sheathed her sword. She closed the bottle and put it back in her pouch. When she looked around the cover of the boulder she saw Ceartas being squeezed. The Wild woman slammed her own skull into his.

Once.

Twice.

Three times.

She let go and Ceartas dropped to the ground a limp sack of flesh.

The Wilder backed up and smiled wickedly with her crooked teeth as she slowly placed her axes back into her hands. Confident in her victory, she walked over to Trodaire and kicked him to the ground. She brought her axe up high.

When she was at her pinnacle, ready to descend, Raven moved from her position and began firing. The five bolts hammered into the savage woman, but not a single shot hit center mass. When Raven got to the edge of the farm she dropped the crossbow and took her throwing axe to cut her other straps to her armor, letting it fall as well.

The Wilder now with a total of nine bolts in her, again smiled wickedly. "So this is the best the Jasian Enclave has to offer?" She was still immune to the pain of the bolts protruding from her body.

Raven looked at the men on the ground, and then returned a smirk back to the barbarous woman. "No, they are just men. No match for a woman's wrath or her revenge."

"You are a coward, female, using ranged weapons thinking you can defeat me. I will kill you just for sport," the wild woman said, bringing up her axes.

Raven countered with a smile just as wicked as her opponent. "I wouldn't have it any other way, bitch. I have been waiting for a rematch with your kind since I was thirteen-winters-old."

The two ran at each other with tremendous speed. The Wilder had reach with her axes over Raven, but that didn't stop the Vadőr. Right when she came within the reach of her rival, Raven dropped to her knees, sliding on the loose ground just under the swings of the two axes aimed for her head. Using her throwing axe in mid-slide, Raven cut the leather strap on the left axe, and then sliced into her target's groin, as she passed through the Wilder's legs.

The Wild Woman barely let out a grunt as the axe bit flesh. She turned with her right axe and came down toward Raven's back. The Vadőr was quick, but not fast enough. Raven felt the burn of fire down her right side, and her grip weakened on her throwing axe. She immediately leaped forward out of range as the second axe caught a few loose hairs from behind. She turned around to see the large woman advancing. The Vadőr deftly scanned her surroundings and saw what she needed to do.

Raven ran toward the Wilder, switching her throwing axe from right to left. Right before the swing from her opponent she leapt on top of a barrel and somersaulted over the monstrosity of a woman. Hitting the ground, she tucked and rolled to the right, coming up with a clear wide target splayed out before her. She threw the axe with unerring accuracy and was rewarded with a solid strike into the beastly woman's back.

With the axe still planted in her back, the green-eyed fury turned around to see Raven standing with her arms and legs apart, looking at her with fierce determination in her own viridian gaze, her hair, cut free, billowing in the highland breeze. Blood trickled down Raven's hip and over her thigh. The wild woman saw the glint of copper strands in the glow of the setting sun.

"A Vadőr, I understand now," she said with a nod. "This is good. When I kill you I will bring back your head to the Strie-kÿr. You are a mighty prize. I will surely be awarded my own hunting party," the feral female said confidently.

Raven smirked. "Not this day." She ran forward toward the woman.

The Wilder, right before Raven tried to use the barrel again, smashed it with both her axes. The Vadőr deftly slid around her opponent, jumped up, and grabbed the throwing axe out of her back. It released from the meat of her muscle with an audible squelch. Before the Wilder could react, Raven twisted to her left and plunged the axe into the right wrist of the behemoth, severing the leather strap and breaking the bone skull that covered her hand. Muscles parted, the feral woman's axe clanged against the hard packed earth.

Enraged, she slammed her dead fist into Raven, dazing her and knocking her backwards. Like a rabid animal, she pulled the axe out of her cleft arm and threw it away from her.

The Wilder attempted to grab the remaining battleaxe with both hands, though the severed tendons made her grip weak. Still, she took advantage of the dazed Vadőr. She swung toward Raven.

Raven felt a burning across her abdomen and then more pain in the bottom of her jaw as she was knocked back against the stone house. Stars danced in her eyes as her lungs yearned for lost breath. She felt something large and unyielding around her neck. She heard the woman before she saw her. "You will die now, Vadőr bitch. But first you will taste pure agony."

Pain coalesced inside her skull like an overfilled waterskin demanding release. It felt like the seams of her very skull were beginning to rupture so that the blood in her head would have a place to go. Her life's essence roared in her ears like a wild tide. Slowly, inexorably, the novas that danced before her eyes began to dull. As Raven was finally starting to black out she frantically reached for her longsword. The wild woman saw her and smiled. "You want to stab me with your stick?"

She moved back and extended her arm, still clutching Raven's throat, squeezing tighter. "Go ahead, it will be the last thing you see, me standing over you as you die – conquered."

The Jasian exactor mustered what little strength she had left and unsheathed the sword and in one fluid motion, she spun the sword and cut around her adversary's arm. The cut was shallow and seemed hardly worth the effort. Raven felt the sword fall from her numb fingers

The other woman laughed, "it's time to die, little bitch." Raven felt her place the axe head into her wound and began to press while tightening her grip around the throat.

Raven howled in agony, but only a tiny wheeze escaped her air-starved lips

Then the pressure was gone! Raven felt herself fall to the ground. Raven coughed as sweet air filled her famished lungs. She gasped like a fish pulled from the sea.

Raven opened her eyes, blood was everywhere, most of it hers. She was light-headed, and knew she didn't have much longer. She looked down at the large woman, who was still awake but not moving. Raven slowly picked her sword off the ground and stumbled, then stood, over the fallen form and weakly smiled. "Oh… you… don't… know what's happening?" she taunted. "This is how you die."

Raven took the sword and slit the woman's throat and then shoved it into the wild woman's left eye socket with all her remaining strength.

The weapon slid through the cavity and stopped at the back of her skull.

Raven left it there, pinned in the brain of the kneeling corpse. She staggered forward, intent on giving help to her comrades, but her legs could not hold her. Her world tilted as she fell to the ground in front of the door of the farm house, and then the Vadőr known as Raven knew no more.

# EPILOGUE

## 1

Raven slowly opened her eyes. A light – muted and dull gently caressed her face. She found herself staring at a white linen ceiling. Beneath her she could feel the coarse fibers of canvas scratching her bare flesh. She woke up lying on a bed in the healing tent of the contingent, she realized. Raven struggled to sit up when one of the female nurses approached. "Milady, please… you must rest." She paid no mind to her and sat up anyways, grunting at the pain in her abdomen.

"So I see that our exactor is up and well," a familiar voice called from the entrance flap of the tent. It was Ceartas, in his now clean armor. He was sporting a three inch scar on the upper right side of his temple.

Raven gave a slight smile, trying to hide the pain she was in as she adjusted to get more comfortable. "How long?" she asked in between breaths.

"A week," the War-Curate answered.

"The others?" she asked a little more comfortable.

Ceartas entered the tent and approached Raven. He grabbed a wooden chair and placed it next to her bed. "Dwyn has quite a few scars, but I got to him in time. In fact, he's out and about I'm sure causing some type of mischief." He reached over and took her hand, "Trodaire is no worse for wear other than his ego. He's been worried about you all week and has been in the practice area trying to better his skill."

Raven adjusted herself again to alleviate some pain on her left side. "What about the monk?" she inquired.

Another voice came from the entrance of the tent. It was deep and gentle and seemed to be full of wisdom. "Thanks to your group, I am alive and well, young maiden."

When she looked over she saw a man dressed in a white gi that bore grey sleeves and was well formed to his body, cinched in place with a black belt. His dark skin was exotic, more than the standard people of Gurgen, Malten perhaps? He still sported the remanants of a bruise across the right side of his face. His black hair was long and in a large pony tail that almost reached his hindquarters. His dark eyes were very mysterious and yet had compassion within them.

She nodded in the man's direction. "Master Ferric, I presume."

He returned the nod. "I am."

Raven looked to Ceartas for direction. "What happened?"

Master Ferric approached and Ceartas stood, giving the monk the chair. He looked at the bedridden exactor and asked, "May I?"

She nodded and he took the seat. Once he adjusted himself he closed his eyes and meditated for a moment. When he opened them, he explained, "I'm sure you have questions, so please permit me to tell you what happened first. During the raid, I made my way toward Norna's in order to keep her at bay."

"She really was a witch, wasn't she?" Raven interrupted, surprising the monk and Ceartas.

"Yes, but not how you think," Ferric replied.

Raven smiled briefly. "I gathered that, based on my own studies and what Maggie and Dwyn told me at Norna's shop."

The monk nodded. "Perceptive." He continued, "I was en-route to the west side of town when I came across the quartet that was slaughtering Brackus' family, so I engaged and took one down. Then Norna and Hynafin joined in the defense of Agot. Apparently I was too late in stopping her. One of the Wildmen said that they knew her human form and cast a magical fireball to take out everyone. I assumed he was some type of a wild shaman. After the explosion the shaman told the others to leave and to head to their rendezvous point. He was going to deal with Norna.

As much as I wanted to help her, I knew that if the Wildmen had more forces, Agot would not survive the night. So I gave chase. Ser Hynafin with Norna and others, including several monks, were the town's best chance in my absence. As long as her potion was in his system, they both had a good chance while I dealt with delaying the reinforcements.

"What do you mean 'human form'?" Raven asked.

Master Ferric sighed and looked down to his hands, "Norna was a dragon."

"Then... the lizard body!" Raven exclaimed.

"She is dead," Ferric said sadly.

Ceartas interjected, "Master Ferric, I am sorry for Norna, but that Wildman was no shaman. He was possessed by an ancient creature that was suffused with magic."

Ceartas looked to Raven, "I 'saw' it when I pulled the last thoughts from the dead Wilder's mind. This *demon,* for no other explanation, could control the actions of people – and it had it's own memories which were – disturbing, and I'm not quite certain I understood that alien mind, then, or now." The purist shuddered, at what he saw in the dark recesses of the Wilder's final thoughts.

Raven took this in. "That explains how it knew Norna from way back when," Raven added. She looked at the Monk. "How old was she?"

Ferric looked down at the ground for a moment then answered, "Six hundred and eight winters; very old."

Ceartas had to ask, "Why was there dragon here in Agot at all?"

"She was lonely," was the simple answer. Ferric continued, "Norna lost her mate many winters before anyone settled here. When people did come to the area she was curious. She put on a human disguise like many dragons do, and made a shop, at first, a trading post if you will. There were only a few farms and a hamlet when I arrived with Hynafin after our adventure with his father," Master Ferric replied. "You already know how quickly this became a boomtown after Agot got sole trading rights with the dwarves."

The two nodded to the monk.

"How did you survive a week?" Raven inquired.

The monk turned to her. "I gave chase and engaged them just outside Agot. I was knocked out by the Wilders in a combined effort on their part. Every time I began to wake, in their custody, they would just knock me out again. In between the two states of consciousness, I did, however hear them say something about possibly taking me to Strie-kÿr. They made camp at the farm, to see if the shaman would return; he was their group leader, in the absence of someone they called - Ambrosia."

Ceartas and Raven locked eyes. Seven winters they'd tracked down that name. Did they finally, *finally* have a solid lead? Master Ferric went on, "When I finally did wake I broke out of the cellar of the farm home you were at. I found your healer doing everything to keep you alive. That is also when I found Norna's and Hynafin's bodies. In order to save you though, we all had to get back here as quickly as we could. I have already dispatched the burial team to the farm and informed the next of kin earlier this week. To be honest I don't know why they kept me alive at all. The Wilders seemed determined to kill everyone else."

Raven looked at Ceartas, "So this attack was really against the Order of the Sacred Fist, then," she stated.

"Looks like it," the healer replied.

"But why? It doesn't make any sense?" Raven pondered aloud.

A sharp pain shot through her and she twinged. The nurse asked everyone to leave to let the patient get her rest. Ceartas smiled as he left, but not before opening the flap for Master Ferric to leave.

## 2

The next few weeks Raven was allowed to leave the healing tent, and she slowly began her therapy to heal the damage done to her. During that time she could see Purist Amháin was unhappy with the healers letting her have leather armor instead of the platemail in order to allow proper healing of her wounds. She was just glad to be out from under its weight. She made sure she was in attendance at the training area, stretching and slowly doing her weapons exercises.

Trodaire was happy to see her and even assisted with her therapy. When he did, she gave him some pointers on how he could combat someone twice his size. He was grateful but still made a suggestive comment or two, "Is this how one can find favor with a Vadőr?" At that, she would just smile and coyly reply, "One never knows…"

One time Purist Amháin heard the banter and chastised her again for such impure thoughts. He then, in order to embarrass her, made mention that because of her impurity, her wounds from her encounter was the Maker's way of showing her that she would never bear child.

It was on the evening of that insult, as the sun was setting on the verdant highlands, casting the hillocks in burnished gold, that she was again away from the camp, by the road she was guarding when this little adventure all began. She looked away from the diminishing globe of orange, towards the mountains in the distance. To home. Sitting on the soft grass next to her were Dwyn and Trodaire, both smoking Spriggan leaf.

"So…we saved the Order of the Sacred Fist?" Dwyn asked.

There was thunder to the south, and Raven watched as the wisps of smoke were pulled quickly away in a tiny squall. Trodaire took a puff on his pipe and spoke, "Guess we did, according to Ceartas." He quickly looked south and back to the others, "I think a storm is coming."

Raven finished her drag on her own pipe, blew out the smoke and then reached into her pouch to produce the small bottle she appropriated from Norna's apothecary. She stared at it for a long while, while the men continued to smoke. Finally she agreed with Trodaire, "Yes, a storm is coming. I can smell it."

Dwyn noticed her brooding as he took a particularly long drag on his pipe. As he exhaled the plume of spicy smoke he confessed, "I'm sorry Amháin was a pain again. I should have warned you he was in the area."

"That's ok, Dwyn. He doesn't bother me anymore," she said, almost wistful.

He noticed the bottle she was ardently staring at, and then carefully looked all around them, like they were hiding a big secret from a parent. Dwyn nodded toward the bottle. "What's that?"

Trodaire looked over and added, "is that one of your Vadőr love potions?"

Raven looked at the black liquid in the bottle. She watched its sheen, almost hypnotized by its hidden power that was only barely realized. She smiled playfully towards Trodaire. "No, no love potion, but it will do."

Dwyn took one final drag on his pipe. "You didn't answer. What is that?"

The Vadőr woman stood up, and emptied her pipe contents onto the aureate stained grass. She placed it and the bottle in securely her pouch. "Freedom, Dwyn," Raven said at last, as she began her walk back toward Agot. "It is freedom."

The two men watched her make her way down the hill, back to town, when another roll of thunder echoed in the distance.

# Experience where it all began in-

## THE WAYFARER PRINCE SAGA-
# STORMWIND

Screams echoed throughout the hillside as Stormwind and Carmella ran to the outskirts of Agot. Carmella yelled for Militär first, and then Rosethorn, but her voice was lost in the din of all the others. People were panic-stricken, running wildly away from the massive lumbering forms that moved between buildings.

Stormwind grabbed the arm of a woman fleeing away in fright. She wheeled on him, swinging and screaming crazily. "Whoa, whoa!" he said as he blocked her attacks. "What's happening? Who's attacking Agot?"

Terror-glazed eyes barely looked at him, only flickering to what lay beyond. "The Wilds," she muttered. "They came from the Wild lands."

Stormwind let go of the woman and let her join the throngs of other terrified townsfolk making their way toward the Order of the Sacred Fist for protection.

He looked between the escaping men and women, trying to eye their attackers. The Wild lands to the south of Agot were an almost forbidden territory. Most trade companies preferred going around the long string of mountains to the southeast. They would rather add scores of days to their journey than to risk the rolling aureate plains of the Wild lands. Creatures of disturbing size and foul ilk brooded within the serene-looking landscape.

Those vile things that lurked within the Wild lands, however, lent strength to the few foolish enough to live within. Men and women held fortified towns within the plains, surviving against all odds. Over the generations it caused the peoples within to change. Like the hard and feral monsters of the land, the men and women, too, became hard and feral. They became fearsome and barbaric, their stature in most cases rising to well over seven feet in height. These hardened peoples relished in the fight, in the violence of survival, and in the victory of life. They were often known as Wild Men, or simply Wilders, and few were ever seen outside of the borders of the Wild lands. If they were, it was often as trackers or mercenaries.

The clash of metal on metal sounded nearby bringing Stormwind out of his thoughts. He looked over in the direction of the noise. The ringing of steel against steel was rhythmic to him, almost soothing. Stormwind felt himself drawn to it. He drew his ornate rapier in a smooth motion and stepped forward. To his surprise, Carmella followed fearlessly by his side, her eyes ripping across the townscape looking desperately for her son and friend.

They rounded the corner to look into the alleyway beyond. Four men were engaged in mortal combat. It was three against one. Two of the men were the Agot guard, one a monk, and the other was indeed a Wild Man.

The Wilder towered over the others, casting them in his shadow. He was at least seven feet tall and almost three feet wide at the shoulders. He wore virtually no armor, nor clothing, instead wearing only the skins and furs of the monsters of the Wilds on his body. Stormwind could make out what looked like Sabertooth Tiger skulls on the massive man's hands, and the skin of a reptile, perhaps alligator, running over the barbarian's knees and feet. His thighs, chest, and arms were bare, showing thick, hardened muscles and a myriad of scars that were bred from countless battles. His face was hidden behind the visage of a basilisk's skull, a terrible lizard that dwelt within the Wild lands. It was said that the beast could kill by its very breath, or even with a look, and this man was wearing it's skull as a trophy. A testament to his skill in combat.

The Wild Man handled the trio of men easily, swinging his cumbersome great axe with ruthless efficiency. The man overmatched the guards before they even engaged him. Within seconds the two were cut down, their life's blood pumping hot spray against the walls of the nearby structures. The Wilder fought through the crimson mire without any regard for having taken the men's lives.

The monk, however, fought on. His skill and speed were an exemplification to the teachings of the Order of the Sacred Fist. The monk dodged the axe blows easily, maneuvering quickly between the openings the Wild Man created, to strike him in a flurry of ruthless efficiency. As Stormwind ran to his aid, he could already see welts forming across the barbarian's body where the monk had struck home. Still the monk's crushing blows did not seem to faze the barbarian in the slightest; if anything, the Wild Man seemed to fight even harder.

Stormwind managed to reach the monk's side just as the giant axe whistled through the air for his head. The nimble Elf deftly avoided the blow and struck with the speed of a cobra, plunging the thin blade up between the Wilder's ribs and piercing his heart.

Hazel eyes stared through the gruesome mask, perplexed. Stormwind understood, for he had seen the look before. The barbarian knew something was wrong, yet he felt only a pinch. Stormwind twisted the blade, opening the wound, and then yanked the sword back, removing it from the giant man's chest. Instantly the Wild Man's bewildered gaze went wide in shock and he fell to his side, dead.

Stormwind turned to the monk. "Quickly ..." he began, but was halted. Also crumpled on the ground was the monk who had been fighting so hard. The great cleave that Stormwind had narrowly avoided had not missed the monk. It had struck true, removing the warrior priest's head from his shoulders. Stormwind felt the bile rise in his throat at the sight of the dismembered head lying only a few scant feet from the body. He turned away. There he saw Carmella staring in agony at the dead monk. She had likely known the man.

The High Elf reached gently toward her and took her olive-skinned hand. "Come on Carmella," he said quietly. "There's nothing we can do. Let's find your son."

The words brought Carmella's gaze away from her fallen compatriot. She nodded to him and said not a single word. Then they were off travelling deeper into Agot, and closer to the heart of violence.

~ ~ ~

They arrived in the market place where Stormwind had first met Carmella only two weeks before. The tables and chairs were now turned over, and it looked as if many townsfolk had barricaded themselves within the tavern. Outside, the Agot Militia fought valiantly against the overwhelming size of the enemy. Everywhere Stormwind looked, the men and even women of both the Order and Agot were fighting for their lives against the monstrous Wild Men.

Like the one that Stormwind had encountered in the alley, many of the other barbarian men were covered in the hides and furs of their conquests as well as the skulls of their triumphant victories. Some of those skulls were even humanoid.

Stormwind rushed into the fray with Carmella close behind. He fought with speed and precision and with a deft agility that even the Wild Men were not prepared for. Within moments, three of the barbarians lay dead at his feet and he prepared to advance on more. Behind him he could hear Carmella screaming for her son within the tavern. No one answered her and Stormwind feared that he knew why: Militär was not there.

Stormwind lined himself up with other members of the militia. "Do any of you know Rosethorn?" he yelled to them as they held back the advance of three more Wilders. The barbarians were learning to fear the sting of his blade and were now more reluctant to recklessly advance on him like before.

"Freckled girl?" one of the guards yelled back behind the overturned table. Stormwind tried to maneuver towards the one who had called out the vague acknowledgement but the Wild Men barred his way.

"Yes," he yelled instead. "Have you seen her?"

A Wild Man roared at Stormwind and swung his axe down to cut the Elf in half. Spittle flew from the gargantuan mouth, flinging outward like small moist projectiles. Stormwind sidestepped both. He leapt into the air and drove his rapier down between the man's clavicle and neck. The blade parted the soft flesh easily and sunk low, piercing multiple organs as it passed through his body. Stormwind removed the sword in the blink of an eye and landed gracefully back on his feet, all in a single fluid motion. The Wilder gurgled as he collapsed to the ground.

The remaining militia killed the other two barbarians and shortly after, the soldier came out from behind the table. "I tried to get her to come into the tavern, but she wouldn't listen."

Carmella, hearing the conversation ran up to Stormwind's side. "Did she have anyone with her, a small child perhaps?"

The soldier nodded. "Aye that she did. 'Fraid she wouldn't listen to me. She headed that way," he finished as he pointed east.

Stormwind looked in the direction the soldier indicated, perplexed. "But that's further away from the monastery. Would she not be trying to get to protection? Wouldn't she be trying to get Militär back to you?" he asked as he looked to Carmella.

"I don't know. She is probably just scared. Stormwind, we have to hurry! Rosethorn is not a monk, she is a local. She does not know how to defend herself. And Militär ..."

Stormwind nodded; he understood. Rosethorn could walk right into a Wild Man ambush and not even see it coming. She would have no way to protect Militär then. He grabbed Carmella's hand, squeezed it once reassuringly, and then headed east through the ravaged town of Agot. Buildings were scarred with the deaths of so many. Blood graffitied the walls wherever they went and bodies littered the streets.

However, it was not a total massacre; far from it. The militia could be heard holding their ground, and for every two Agot corpses they found, they found one Wild Man. The barbarians were taking casualties, too. It was only a matter of time before the Wilders would have to declare the battle a rout and withdraw. Stormwind did not think Rosethorn and Militär had that kind of time though.

They looked in every house they passed by and Carmella would call out to the two of them. Still he had not heard a response from either. Nevertheless, one thing he did notice was that they were encountering the Wilders far less frequently. It looked as if the eastern end of the town had been the first to feel the effects of the raid and now the core of the Wild Man advance had held firm in the center of town. It made it easier to search for Carmella's son, and if Militär were around, he would find him.

The two reached the edge of town. Beyond, all that Stormwind could see were farms and tilled fields. If Rosethorn and Militär were cutting through the farmland, Stormwind's keen elven sight would be able to see them but as it was, there was no one to be found. Everyone that was not fighting had fled to the monastery to the west. He turned and looked to the woman whose child he was trying to save. "Did Rosethorn know the farmers well? Would she take Militär to a barn perhaps?" he asked, and then turned to look at the tracks on the ground.

He already knew the answer before she said anything, though. Fresh tracks were only coming in; none were leaving. The tracks inward were also massive depressions that he had gathered came from the footfalls of the Wild Men. There was nothing so small that it denoted that it came from a child or a young woman. Still he waited for Carmella's answer.

"No," she remarked. "Perhaps we missed them somehow," she said with a reserve of calm Stormwind was amazed she had.

"They could have doubled back towards the monastery. Perhaps someone convinced Rosethorn to head there?"

The High Elf watched as the dark-haired beauty bit her lower lip in frustration. "Perhaps," she agreed.

Stormwind began to turn back when suddenly he saw a flicker of movement. The Elf reacted on impulse, pushing Carmella out of the way and diving to the side just as three shards of ebony stone tore through the wooden fencing that they had just been standing near.

Stormwind ended his dive in a roll and came to his feet, his ornate rapier ready. Carmella, however, was not as graceful when she hit the ground.

Stormwind's cerulean eyes scanned the cluster of houses behind him. Carmella and he had just looked in every one and they were empty. From where had the attack come? Then he saw it: the silhouette of a woman in a doorway some twenty feet away. How had he missed that? He heard a chanting sound as she raised her hands once more. Instinct forced him to spin away from her and around the corner of a nearby home. Brick and mortar exploded outward from the edge of the house as another trio of sharp obsidian shards ripped through the building, as if it had no more consistency than wet paper.

He knew what it was then: Magic. The assailer was a sorceress of some kind.

"Krake, finish him," he heard a vaguely familiar voice say from around the corner.

Stormwind pushed himself up against the wall and slowly crouched. His gut told him that he should flank around the building and try to attack the assailers from behind, but as he glanced to Carmella lying prone on the ground he knew he could not leave her behind.

Then a large bone-plated leg stepped into his view of the fallen monk. Stormwind followed it upward to the largest human he had ever seen in his life.

The man had to be close to seven and a half feet tall, his shoulder span reaching almost four feet across. Thick heavy muscle rippled across the huge Wild Man's body through pockets of leather and fur that were patchworked amidst his towering frame. The skulls of basilisks resided on each shoulder, and his dark grey orbs stared down at Stormwind through the skull of an armor-plated crown of a gorgon. Two long horns rose off on both sides of the skull and jutted forward like hooked javelins. Stormwind could see a tangled black beard sticking out from beneath the gorgon mask.

"You must be Krake," he said dryly as the Wild Man roared at him and swung a colossal poleaxe with both hands. The agile Elf easily rolled away from the hulking monstrosity of a man before him and came to his feet once more almost six feet away.

Krake spun around instantly, rolling the poleaxe around easily with the skill of a master. Stormwind looked at the long weapon with a well of fear growing in the pit of his stomach. The poleaxe was over six feet in length with an axe head, a haft of a hammer, and spike tip across the top. It was a versatile weapon and one that hindered the Elf. The barbarian had range and size on Stormwind, and the Elf needed to be close to be effective.

Krake swung the poleaxe in a wide arc, Stormwind barely managing to duck out of the way of the curved blade, when the immense warrior instantly followed through with a crushing slam of his hammer. Stormwind narrowly escaped the pulverizing attack as the hammer head slammed into the cobblestone road, shattering the smooth stones into fragmented slivers and dust.

Stormwind attempted to gain his footing but the Wild Man vigorously advanced. The Elf backpedaled frantically as axe fall followed a swing of a hammer, followed by the stab of the spear tip. It was as if there was no escaping the overpowering goliath. Finally, the deft Elf managed to flip over a small fence to grant him a modicum of room before the Wilder shattered it, too, with a swing of the hammer. Stormwind could not believe the man's speed and endurance for his size. It seemed inhuman!

The Wilder pushed forward, confidence gleaming in his dark glare as he forced Stormwind into retreat again and again. Stormwind thought for sure that the Wild Man was invincible, when he made his first mistake.

As he stabbed forward, he kept the hammerhead facing his opponent and the axe away. Stormwind realized the strategy, for If the Elf dodged to the outside, as the Wilder expected, he could follow through with a sweep attack from the axe, effectively hamstringing the Elf. Stormwind was not going to give him the luxury. When the piece came forward again, instead of dodging to the side, he moved forward.

He spun wide letting the sharp spike slide along the inside of his armor. As he came around he caught the hammer haft and used it as leverage to hurtle himself forward. Within the Wild Man's perimeter and against the weapon, the massive man was defenseless. With all his strength, he stabbed forward. His thin blade perforated the seams of the Wilder's muscled flesh and drove completely through his body, erupting in a crimson explosion as the tip exited his back.

To Stormwind's surprise, the Wild Man did not so much as grunt. Instead, with amazing willpower, Krake dropped his poleaxe and instead grabbed Stormwind, who was so close to the goliath he could not escape in time.

Krake's hands locked onto Stormwind's shoulders, binding his arms in place. With unbelievable strength, he lifted Stormwind from the ground. The grip on his arms was excruciating. Stormwind tried to hold onto his rapier but found the lock on his arms too tight and felt his grip ripped away.

Stormwind knew that things had taken a turn for the worse, but still he did not relent. As the hulking monstrosity squeezed down on him, crushing the air from his lungs, the Elf kicked as hard as he could against the man's flank. If the Wild Man noticed at all, it did not even register. Krake lifted Stormwind up so that the Elf was looking through the eyeholes of the gorgon skull to the man underneath. It was a visage of death. He knew this was the end, yet he remained defiant. With all the power he could muster, he spit into the eyehole.

Krake drove the skull helmet down on Stormwind's head. Searing pain and bright light exploded all around and everything began spinning. He felt the crushing blow again and the light was now replaced with stars. Then he was falling.

The ground rushed up to greet him and he slammed down hard on his side with a cry of pain. The world spun and swerved before him and lights danced all around. He felt hot fluid pouring liberally across his head and down his face. He looked up at the monster above him.

Pain ran through his body like lightning, coursing from his neck down to his toes. Still he watched as the Wild Man slowly reached down to his own abdomen and removed Stormwind's rapier. He made no sound and Stormwind could only watch as the cruor-covered blade slid wetly from the barbarian's body. When the tip finally emerged, a red gout of blood followed it. It was then that Krake grunted. He put his hand over the crimson-drenched wound and threw Stormwind's rapier down.

The Elf tried to move, but his body would not respond. He could only watch as Krake picked up the poleaxe once more. He arced the axe head towards Stormwind's neck, and with one hand raised the weapon for a felling blow. The blade began to race downward.

"Wait!" a woman's voice called.

The blade stopped only inches from Stormwind's face. He stared at the glinting metal hovering so closely above him.

Suddenly a freckled female's hand came into view as she pushed the weapon away from his face. She bent over and smiled wickedly down at him, her green eyes glittering in triumph. "Well … well … well … what an unexpected surprise? And to think I thought it was actually the Agot Militia giving my Wilders such a hard time. I should have figured it to be a High Elf."

He watched helplessly as another Wild Man walked by with an unconscious Militär hanging limply from his shoulder. His gaze fell back to the woman as tears began to stream out of his eyes in shock. She stood up, "Goodbye, Stormwind."

~

# IMPORTANT NAMES AND TERMS

**Agot**- A small highland town of humans that acts as a trading hub between Ethens and the rest of the continent.

**Ambrosia**- A faceless sorceress who has wreaked havoc upon the Jasian Enclave for nearly a decade.

**Aodhfin Bray**- Purist Commander of the 105th Northern contingent.

**Curate**- Female magicians within the Jasian Enclave who use Creative magic solely to heal.

**Dahonin Amháin**- Purist and second-in-command of the 105th Northern contingent. Has a personal disliking for Exactor Raven.

**Dakhym**- True name of the Dark Elves.

**Dakoria**- Nation of Dark Elves. Ruled by the Singh Imperium.

**Drachen**- The Vadőr term for dragon.

**Dwyn Lani**- Human Exactor and a thief. He excels at hiding in plain sight, and has a longstanding friendship with Raven.

**Ethens**- Located deep below the Lugos Mountains, it is the last dwarven stronghold remaining on the continent.

**Exactor**- Contractors whose duty it is to complete the missions that the Church cannot openly admit to doing, or if they need an expendable asset. Often reformed criminals or liberated slaves.

**Featherset**- Capital of the Shemma.

**Ferhym**- True name of the Wild Elves.

**Fermania**- Nation of Humans. Governed by the Seafarer's Caucus and ruled by Countess Helena Kavon.

**Gnome**- Small humanoids with only four digits per hand. They have childlike proportions, but the males tend to be uncharacteristically hairy. Are extremely curious and are arguably the most technologically advanced of all the species of Kuldarr.

**Goldhym**- True name of the High Elves.

**Gurgen**- Religious nation state controlled by the Jasian Enclave. Answers to the Supreme Pontiff.

**High Province**- Nation of High Elves. Ruled by the Trimora dynasty.

**Hym**- Often referred to as Elves. Lithe humanoids that are magically attuned to nature. They adapt to their natural settings over time, even taking on some of elements features. Renowned for their beauty and sharp-pointed ears.

**Jaës**- Capital of Oganis, sometimes referred to as the Red City due to the nature of its stonework.

**Jasian Enclave**- Most powerful religious conglomerate in the world of Kuldarr. Worships and preaches the word of the Maker.

**Kii' Aur**- True name of the Scales.

**Lefhym**- True name of the Wood Elves.

**Loach Hynafin**- One of the founders of Agot.

**Lugos Mountains**- Small mountain range that divides the nations of High Province and Malten.

**Maggie**- A small young woman who works for Norna Dewin at Dewin's Spiritual Concoctions and Goods.

**Malten**- Desert nation ruled entirely by Archmages.

**Norna Dewin**- Proprietor of Dewin's Spiritual Concoctions and Goods. Rumored to be a witch.

**Oganis**- Nation of the Scales. Ruled by the Kii' Aur Hegemony.

**Òrain Ceartas**- Unique Purist capable of using healing magic. Often refered to as a War-Curate.

**Order of the Sacred Fist**- Nestled in the rolling hills of the Agonthill Highlands sits a monastery who's occupants have one simple goal; physical perfection.

**Purist**- A culture of warrior-priests devoted to violently defending and spreading the word of their god, the Maker, and their nation of Gurgen. They are predominantly Human.

**Raven**- Exactor and sole Tracer for the 105th Northern contingent whose skills are invaluable. Self-proclaimed Vadŏr woman, she is hot-headed and regularly pushes the boundaries of tolerance from her Purist leadership.

**Scales**- A race of bi-pedal intelligent caiman responsible for impressive ship-making, and unique sea-faring vessels of war.

**Ser**- An honorific address used as a formal prefix in place of a first name. It is male dominant only, and popular in use in the nations of Gurgen, Halsbren, and the High Province.

**Shemma**- Largest forested region on Kuldarr. It also contains the Wood Elven empire of the same name. It is so large it is considered its own nation.

**Spriggan**- Smaller than a gnome, Spriggans look like very young human children with some noticable exceptions. They have only three fingers and toes on their hands and feet, all clawed. They also have tails, and on top of their heads are dense rows of quills.

**Stormwind**- The adopted High Elven son of the Lefhym empire. Next in line for succession to High Chieftain, and renowned vagabond and adventurer.

**Strie-kÿr**- Mountain stronghold of the Wilder people.

**The Wilds**- nestled between two mountain ranges is a land of verdant valleys where the most fearsome creatures of Kuldarr all make their home.

**Tilliatemma**- a series of islands on a massive fresh water lake deep underneath the Broken Teeth Mountains. It is the capital of Dakoria.

**Tracer**- An individual who has the unique talent of locating missing products, parcels, persons, etc.

**Trodaire Casein**- Human fighter. Newest Exactor in the 105th Northern contingent. Seems slightly infatuated with Raven.

**Vadőr**- A group of nomadic tribal women who live in the mountain regions, and excel in the art of mortal combat.

**War-Curate**- Rare male Curates capable of engaging in battle as well as healing.

**Wilder**- Wild men are humans whose ancestry have made a dark pact with one of the deities of old giving them monstrous size and strength.

~

Learn where Purist Commander Aodhfin Bray went off to in – Stormwind – book one of the Wayfarer Prince Saga, available at Amazon.com, on Amazon Kindle, and at www.AuthorJayErickson.com

For more on the exploits of the Exactor named Raven look for – Veil of Resolve – book two of the Mark of the Raven (coming soon).

If you enjoyed this novel, please take a moment and review it favorably. Every bit helps.

Thank you.

J. P. Strohm
*Author*

# ABOUT THE AUTHOR

J.P. STROHM lives in Indiana with his wife Susan. He has been a fan of the medieval period with its legendary stories and histories. Mr. Strohm has served in the United States Air Force for over twenty five years. He is an avid gamer and continues to captivate people with his stories of adventure in worlds unknown.

# Jay Erickson
## *The Blood Wizard Chronicles*

*"Pariah* is a fine example of intricate world-building with an interesting take on the standard fantasy tropes. A complex tale featuring adult themes and intriguing, relatable characters, it's a promising beginning to the *Blood Wizard Chronicles* series."
-C.S. Marks, author of *The Elfhunter Series*

## PARIAH
978-1-942958-05-5

## RECREANT
978-1-942958-08-6

"A dense and violent series opener seeded with events of grand consequence."
-Kirkus Reviews

"Voice and Writing Style 5 out of 5!"
-23rd Annual Writer's Digest Self-Published Book Awards

And don't miss
## BARROW OF LIES
978-1-942958-14-7

www.authorjayerickson.com

# Anastasia M. Trekles
## *Chronicles of M'gistryn*

"Anastasia M. Trekles takes readers on an epic adventure in her debut novel Core. Told from the perspective of multiple characters, Core borrows familiar elements of our world to create a thrilling fantasy filled with intrigue, action, and romance. The characters are engaging with witty banter and personalities that sprawl across the page. Trekles masterfully guides readers through worlds rich with lore, but never bogs down the prose with too much description or exposition. She has a keen sense of a modern reader's imagination and deftly transports us through time and space. Trekles has a deep understanding of the fantasy genre and weaves a tale that will satisfy anyone who appreciates a great story told well. This novel establishes the foundation for a series of books and invites a reader back for more."

-S.E. White, author of *A Murder of Crows*

## CORE
978-0-9964311-0-1

## ASCENT
978-0-9964311-2-5

"Simply amazing! Characters who actually behave like adults! This novel is highly recommended!"
-J.P. Strohm, author of *Broken Order*
www.zelda23publishing.com